SOCIAL PRESSURE

By Audrianna M. Brownell

Description: First Edition | Denver: Audrianna Brownell, 2025 | Series: [Greek Life; 1] | Blurb; Elle O'Hare holds her gavel tight. As President of her sorority, Kappa Sigma Iota, she already has a full schedule as a sophomore, with classes, meetings, and dealing with the presidents from the other fraternities and sororities on the Conifer Valley University campus.

Identifiers: ISBN (Paperback): 979-8-9915002-4-1 ISBN (ebook): 979-8-9915002-5-8

Subjects: AC: College, Fraternity and Sorority, etc.—Fiction. | Romance, Contemporary, etc. —Fiction. | Sorority—Fiction. | Greek Organizations—Fiction.

Printed in the United States of America.

Jordan, I love you because we started off in the most unconventional way but our souls fought to forge forever. Sorority brought me *you*, and for that I will never truly speak too ill of our time. Even as we navigated which parts of this story seemed too far-fetched.

To my sisters: I am sorry ladies, but many of these exaggerations either happened directly to me or were a fabrication of real life tales from other Greek members' lips. I wish I could make it all up, but alas you gave me so much good material for inspiration.

Dear Readers,

Social Pressure is a fictional story about young people with real life issues and the immense stress that can be placed on college students who are a part of organized organizations like Sororities and Fraternities. Therefore this novel includes heavy topics surrounding mental heath— specifically anxiety and depression, suicide and self harm, hazing, and anger management disorders. Therefore, some aspects of Social Pressure may be triggering for some readers.

I wish everything in this tale was purely imagined, and not at all similar to a true lived experience but that wouldn't be realistic in depicting the lives of members within these organizations. Even though scenes and characters in Social Pressure are all fictitious and imagined, they are all inspired by true events and authentic beings.

Chapter One

A Not So Random Wednesday in November

ELLE

The urge to click my pen repeatedly is killing me. Every second that the President of Sigma Rho Beta drowns on and on about his newest and brightest idea is absolutely annoying. He has no idea how the school is going to react to the proposal for a new "All Greek Space", because he does nothing but think about his own brotherhood and how they can have one more thing over the other students on campus.

No, he has no idea that the board of directors, overseeing Greek life's activities, isn't going to approve this proposal, because he of course hasn't included the other Greek presidents in his plans. Which is why, I, along with the other seven chosen electors for each group that make up the Greek Life at Conifer Valley University, in Conifer Valley Colorado, now sits listening to his boring speech. About how the school needs to give back to the largest philanthropist on campus. Which of course is an exaggeration to overshadow all the negative aspects that Greek life has contributed to the student body. Ironically, his fraternity are the ones who cause the most damage, and the majority of the anger I also hold for all Greek life's men.

Greek life at Conifer Valley University is not your typical Greek college experience. There were no houses or generations of alumni. No, the university had only accepted Greek life onto their campus ten years ago. Sigma Rho Alpha— or SRB as they called themselves— was the first all male Fraternity on campus. So their president, Trent Turner, has more than enough balls to stand in front of the small fluorescent lit meeting room, and spout on about how he is going to "change the trajectory of Greek Life for the better".

The slide changes on the monitor at the front of the room and Trent continues to beam brighter, whilst explaining that "community is important to growing our organizations". He holds little care for the size of the other groups on campus.

An exaggeration?

Maybe, but I can't quite believe he doesn't have an ulterior motive to wanting a private space for the Greeks to spend their time. If Trent did his research he would note that the school already has spaces like the one he is suggesting available to students.

"Is the Student Life offices not sufficient?" asks Holden, the Director of the Student Life offices, adorned in his navy blue collared shirt and gray pressed slacks as he scribbles notes on his yellow pad— hardly looking up to see Trent's reaction to his interruption. His young, chiseled features are decorated in a sea of freckles, all matching his dark brown eyes and dark shaggy hair. For a campus employee he is definitely considered *hot*. His good looks and the fact that he had also been a member of Greek Life at his undergraduate university leads to the respect he has gained from all the presidents and other students of Conifer Valley.

Trent Turner, on the other hand, is exactly as you'd expect when picturing a Fraternity president. Handsome, authoritative, and extremely pretentious. So, Trent's nose crinkles momentarily at the question before explaining that it is in the slides coming up.

Trent had grown up in the high mountains of Colorado and was born to a long line of SRB's. Born into silver and bleeding out navy, SRB's official colors. His pride is more than evident.

I don't hate him for these reasons. I hate him because outside this room he is exactly as you would assume a fraternity man would be— a partier, expert beer pong player, and ultimate playboy amongst the newer Greek life members. Especially the freshly initiated women of my sorority Kappa Sigma Iota (KSI).

I sigh slightly, watching Trent ramble on, while I mentally tally off all my tasks for the day. I still need to type up my report for this week's meeting, so I can send it to my Scribe for the official minutes. Then I need to email the Social Chair back about her wanting to drop her position, again. I also have a one on one meeting with Holden and I have no idea what he could possibly want, because my sorority is always in line with everything.

We meet the deadlines for event space reservations, hold our health risk and safety seminars monthly, and continually work with the campus's community service representative to excel at hours served at Conifer Valley's local community food bank.

Trent finally finishes his presentation with a brief statement explaining that the Greeks need a separate space from the other students in order to "grow community relations".

"Isn't that what socials are for?" asks Alicia Hawkins, the president of Zeta Phi Nu (or "Zeta Phi" as they call themselves). Another Sorority on campus, one that prides themselves on excellent grades and shiny blonde hair. I don't have anything against her or her sorority either, I just don't really care about all the superficial fights between the Greek organizations. The petty arguments that circle around campus, dividing the chapters, and pitting them against one another all seem extremely juvenile to me. Thus only amplifying the notions that the fraternity men continue to spit— labeling the Zeta Phi's as the prettiest sorority while the KSI's are a bunch of nerds.

Their words. Not mine.

Alicia is pretty, the conventional kind of beautiful that results from good genes and the gift of natural blonde spiral curls often seen on women from oceanside states like hers. Her skin is still a deep tan from the sunny summer laying on the Florida beaches.

I like my sorority, because they are authentic and all have our differences visually and otherwise. I also made great friends going through the recruitment process, and felt welcomed immediately. That's how someone was supposed to pick a sorority— not based on the fraternities labels.

"This space will give the social chairs a *free space* on campus to host events," Trent boasts, as he takes his seat next to me. Scribbling down the question, like he plans to reiterate them— exactly as Alicia had asked- to his chapter members in their next formal meeting.

"That sounds great to me," chimes Carl Giffin, the president of Alpha Epsilon Chi. His perfect large lipped bright white smile flashing against his deep brown skin. His fraternity is the newest on campus and is, not so secretly, considered the SRB's "buddy fraternity".

Of course this all sounds like a great idea to everyone because all they seem to worry about is where to have fun, where to socialize, and where to get laid.

"The university already allows for free event space reservations." I say, not looking away from the window. Students bustle by, completely unaffected by the mundane activities of running a student organization.

No one responds, until Carl speaks again, giddy as always. "We could host a grand opening right before Rush."

Alicia's brown eyes find me as I gaze back at the group. I really don't want to re-explain the differences between the Fraternity and Sorority recruitment processes *again*. Basically, the Fraternity's have a more laissez-faire way of recruiting members, so they are able to use the outdated term "Rush", and they can simply ask a person to join, making a man feel beyond chosen and they will be initiated within the week. I'm not one hundred percent certain how it all happens so fast, just that it isn't that simple for the women's organizations.

"It's called recruitment for us," I huff, turning my gaze to him, "not rush."

"All the chapters will need to be in agreement if I am to bring the idea to the Board of Directors. You don't need to decide today, as we are out of time. We will pick up the conversation again next week," states Holden as he stands. Folding up his leather pad, before sliding a sheet of paper to each of us. "This is the proposal, please bring it up in your chapter meetings so we can have some official opinions from each organization."

He is only making us do this because it is procedure. We each represent our chapters in this setting, but are required to get an overall chapter vote at the weekly meetings we each hold.

Meeting's make up the majority of the tasks each president has to do. There are the president's meetings of course, like this one. Then the Executive board meeting with the governing members of each chapter, the event coordinator meetings with the school, the meetings with their chapter advisors, then the ones with Holden in the Student Life Office.

All of which happen weekly. In addition, we attend other meetings as well, such as the Executive board meetings hosted by the Vice Presidents, then the Panhellenic and Interfraternal Council ones held between the organizations, and finally the one on ones with other chapter representatives.

One would think that is a lot, piled on one person, along with attending college classes, but that isn't even all of the meetings. There are also the small meetings we each have, that come up more unexpectedly. Like the one I am going to be required to have with our social chair if she continues to threaten to quit, and only weeks before her event— her quitting would be a huge burden.

"Elle," Holden glances in my direction, as I scramble to put my notes into my black faux leather tote bag. He remains patient while I struggle squeezing in the paper next to my constitutional binder and folders for each of my meetings, forcing it down next to my small silver laptop. "Don't forget to see me in my office."

"Of course," I reply, with a tight lined smile. I don't have class for a few more hours. My schedule was selected solely with these meetings in mind. I told my advisor it was for lunch and studying, but really I need to be strategic to be a successful president. So it's all morning and late afternoon classes for me. Everyone else focuses on school first, then Greek life. I, on the other hand, always think about Greek life, and pray that I do well enough in class to pass with the grades that I need to hold my position. Ironic that I ran a sorority labeled as nerds, when I myself only excel at being President (or Archon as we call it) of said sorority.

Everyone funnels out of the small meeting room and into the grand Student Life Office, filled with plastic feeling leather couches and large glass tables for studying. Most students are decorated in their best greek letters, sprawling in intermixed groups— laughing and socializing. Other students sit further away from the Greek students, in their own miniature groupings visibly studying or playing cards. Most of the faces I recognize, even the non Greek Life students. The school's government office was also attached to the space, so the place is always alive with buzzing student led activities. It's a sanctuary for all; there's plenty of space for the members of Greek Life.

Trent— who is already meeting up with his SRB brothers— buzzes within the congratulatory murmurs about his presentation. My eyes roll, as I hike my tote higher onto my shoulder, propelling my feet to turn away from the crowd and continue down the hall to Holden's office in the back of the large space.

As my feet reach the small lip on the carpet that separates the two spaces, just past the door frame, a large man barrels backwards. Hitting me with his entire body and knocking my bag off my shoulder. The pain that rocks through the bridge of my nose makes me reach up instinctively, and the fury that wraps around my entire soul is combustible.

"What the fuck?" I grumble, as the stranger lunges to assess where he has slammed his shoulder into my face.

"Oh my god!" his voice is all genuine concern. "I didn't see you there, I am so so sorry."

"It's fine." I grumble, as the sensation of liquid runs down my throat. I shoot my chin towards the ceiling.

"Oh god," he curses again. "You're bleeding."

I pinch the bridge of my nose to stop it from causing more of a scene. "I said I'm fine." My voice pinches while I hold my nostrils tight. I realize quickly that I haven't even looked at the man who has *shoulder checked* me, until a white facial tissue waves in front of my eyes.

His blond hair flutters across his pale ivory face as he holds the white paper close to my nose, his soft hazel eyes fixated on it, like he is a doctor or something. Which he clearly isn't, because he's wearing a dark red tee shirt with the name of a band I don't recognize and black jeans decorated with holes. His entire presence is alluring, but he is in fact a complete stranger, touching my nose with one hand and grasping my elbow with the other. His calloused fingers running circles on my skin and sending tingles down my spine.

"I'm fine," I pull from his grasp, the sting of the interaction flaring the pain in my nose further. I assess the tissue in my palm and stride past him. Crimson splotches look up at me as I strut into Holden's office and I sit in the chair next to the door, before replacing the light paper to my nostrils.

"Elle?" Holden asks, watching me as I pull my meeting folders out and onto my lap. Fiddling through with one hand to find this meeting's tab. "What happened to your nose?"

"Some, *rhino of a man,* trampled me in the hall."

"Just now?" Holden asks, handing me another tissue. This one comes away less red, so I sniffle and suck in a deep breath, before tipping my head back to rest on the wall behind me.

"Holden?" a deep familiar voice startles my eyelids open. Standing next to me in the open door frame is the man who had just assaulted my nose.

I let out a disgruntled sigh.

"Oh there you are. Sorry Holden." The stranger says before kneeling down, resting his large hands on the edge of my wooden framed chair. "One second."

"I am beyond sorry, um.." He stops, his eyes searching my face. "What's your name?"

I clasp my arms at my chest, trying to avoid our skin touching again. Before scoffing at him. He isn't serious is he?

"Elizabeth." I never use my full name, but whenever someone asks me to introduce myself it always comes out. Or when I sign my name at the top of a test, always my full name. Every teacher and hockey couch always called me Elle— because it was easier to remember— and at some point I simply just stopped correcting people.

"I am beyond sorry, Elizabeth." The man's deep stare never leaves me, but the idea of looking and finding his gold flecked eyes staring back at me makes me uncomfortable, so I keep my eyes on Holden— who seems more entertained then upset by this intrusion. "Let me make it up to you. Let me take you to dinner?"

"What?" I huff, now facing him. "We don't even know each other."

The man smiles at this, a bright white smile of perfect teeth, and a small dimple forms in his left cheek before saying, "That wasn't a no."

"No."

"Oh, Elizabeth please?" he grasps his palms together, balancing on the balls of his feet in his black and white sneakers.

"I have a boyfriend," I say, finding Holden's brows raised at my statement.

"No you don't." The man's voice makes my gut flutter.

My mouth pops open as I turn to him again, "Yes I do."

"No," he smiles again, his cheeks reddening slightly, "Everyone in Greek life knows everything about everyone else, and it's my job to know everything about the other chapters."

"Then absolutely not." I huff, turning away from this annoying man again. I made a rule long ago that I wouldn't be caught dead dating a fraternity man. Or fucking one. It is too messy, and I have enough on my plate already.

"Fine," he stands and retreats from the room, thus ending our sparring match.

"I see you've met Devin," Holden smiles and crosses an ankle over his pressed pant knee.

"Who is he exactly?" I am a bit astonished that Holden would rather gossip about the Greeks than discuss the meeting's topics.

"That's SRB's new social chair."

"Great," I say, rolling my eyes, "is he relevant to this meeting?"

"No." Holden laughs before beginning his questioning on my chapters happenings and my personal ability to handle my class load and responsibilities of being president.

I volley every question as usual, and we finish our meeting in record time. I realize I had only thought about Devin twice. Once because I thought he'd storm back in, and again when I re-emerge into the Student Life office— worried he'll barrel into me.

"Elle!" hollers my sister, Scarlett, decorated in our sororities colors— a pastel pink crew neck and green KSI stitched letters across her chest. Her dirty blonde hair in a high ponytail. "Come sit with us."

Luckily, I have a few more hours to spend socializing before I need to head to class. My sisters will be a perfect distraction.

Chapter Two

Wednesday

DEVIN

"So she's a senior?" I ask, trying not to make Trent mad.

"No," he scoffs, "somehow she's become president as a sophomore."

"That's impressive." I say, chewing down on the pizza that I had grabbed on the way past one of the University's many cafeterias.

Trent had insisted we have, what he calls, "a walk and talk" meeting. He has many places to be with his full class load of business courses and being President of our Frat. (Sigma Rho Beta), so it was the least I could do, having little to no where to be myself.

I only take classes three times a week and never before noon. Today is the first day I've ever come to campus "early". According to Trent, it is good for me to be seen in the student life office. Texting Holden this morning to jump on his schedule is the only reason I am here now. Holden didn't officially agree to our meeting but

Trent had previously mentioned a grace period after their presidents meeting.

That was all before I slammed into *her*. Elizabeth O'Hare— or Elle as everyone else seemed to know her by. With her bright blue eyes and dark brown shoulder length hair framing her lightly tanned face in the cutest bangs I had ever seen on someone. The tiny button nose that I had almost broken was decorated in an array of light brown freckles that make me want to trace over each with my finger tips. Even with flooded eyes and crinkled features she was breathtaking. The reality of our altercation immediately struck me into a panic. Hurting a woman was unforgivable. I couldn't be like him.

Offering to take her out seemed like the perfect way to apologize and to keep my mind off of all my responsibilities, and even with her refusal I would continue to try. Women like her are worth it. Trent wanted nothing to do with her— instead diverting conversations to the brotherhood.

Specifically, the ideas for the social themes, so I listed them off for him in between bites of pizza, until the massive building that houses the School of Business came into view.

"So bowling, or go cart races." I stammer as Trent types away on his phone. He hardly seems to care what I choose for an activity, as long as the event is successful. Unsure what to say, my mind trickles back to Elle's beautiful blue irises. Icey blues that filled with moisture as she held firm not to cry in front of a stranger. Based on the things Trent had said, it seems she doesn't ever show much emotion in front of anyone.

"Why do you care so much about the Ice Queen anyways?" Trent asks before turning to face me, the stone building casting a shadow over us. He glances at his watch then back at me, as I chomp another mouthful of pepperoni.

"IOntkNOW." I stammer over the chunks of cheesy dough and rich sauce in my mouth.

"Seriously, Willard." Trent huffs, his dark black hair barely moving in the breeze because he styles so much product into it. "Don't talk with your mouth full."

"Sorry," I clear my throat at the sound of my last name, and throw the crinkled parchment covered in grease into the trash near the door.

"I took a chance on you letting you in, Mec." Trent says before gripping my shoulder. His dark brown eyes, always stern, tracing over my features. I learned a few years back that he uses the French slang— that he learned abroad— as a term of endearment. We are of similar height but my days playing soccer makes me slightly broader. "We've known each other for a long time, so I know you can be a good SRB brother, but don't worry about KSI's president. That's my job."

"Okay." I say hoping to sound casual, even though the words *my job*, and *ice queen* are circling in my head. Elle was feisty, but an ice queen seems a bit harsh, and Trent holding any possession over her makes my skin twitch. Didn't he have a girlfriend?

"Just focus on the social with the KSI nerds in two weeks." Everyword out of Trent's mouth was meant to be a joke. I knew that. He knew that, but everyone else often missed the sarcasm.

"What's wrong with being a nerd?" I ask, confused why he feels the need to put down the entire sorority in one fell swoop.

"Right," he scoffs, "I got to go, Mec. See you tonight at Le Cougar Trap?"

"Sure." I say, agitated at the name of the row of town homes that Trent and a few other brother's live in. They again have labeled the houses the "Le Cougar Trap" as a joke because the fraternity's chapter mascot is a mountain lion, but it feels dirty in my mind.

As I stand watching Trents retreat, my phone buzzes alive in my pocket, I don't need to look at it to see who is on the caller ID. I know it is my dad. The only person who calls anyone. Everyone texted nowadays and he knows how much I hate to talk on the phone.

I turn, striding back up the large hill, unsure where to go. I'm certainly not going to my College Algebra class. The entire class was a waste of time. One I would've tested out of, but I didn't want to be placed in a higher level or required to work harder.

The library glistens in the sun, with its magnificently large clock at the top of its tall tower, beckoning me towards it. School isn't hard for me, just fucking boring. Which is one of the reasons I transferred to Conifer Valley University, because it is small and classes are easy to make up with winter courses or online. I will be able to swoop in on test day and pass the class, and if I didn't then I'd have an excuse to stay over break. One simple click would add it to my schedule, and away from home was my preferred place to be.

A familiar face, under a tight round brown bun, flutters past and I turn on my heels. "Lacy!"

"Devin, I can't talk now I'm late for class." Lacy continues her stroll down the hill while I chase her.

"Wait, you haven't texted me back about the social event in two weeks."

"Right," Lacy hums as she removes her earbuds, not slowing her pace. "Well, I just texted Elle, our president, and told her I quit."

"Quit?" I stammer, trying to glance at her face to see if she is joking while I jog beside her.

"Yeah, I thought it was going to be all fun, you know. Like parties and such, planning the Spring Formal. Turns out that's an entirely different chair. Can you believe it?"

"Uh, yeah." I stammer as I try to keep up with her and her drawling voice. "Who's the new chair then?"

"I don't know," she stops in front of the glass doors leading into the business building, "guess we'll vote on Sunday or something."

I pull the door open for her to enter, staring into the space she just vacated. Extremely confused on how I am to plan a social with a sorority that now has no social chair to help plan it.

My phone begins to buzz as I make my ascent up the hill, again. This time I can't ignore it, I need to get my mind off the fraternity business and classes.

"Dad?" I say, hesitantly.

"Why aren't you in class?" my dads deep baritone voice penetrates through the tiny speaker, sending a jolt through my spine.

"I just got out." I say, hoping to sound convincing in my lie.

"What class ends at 1:47 pm."

"Uh," I should say any name of a class, but they all leave my mind as he speaks.

"I don't pay for you to fuck around, son." I bit my tongue, anticipating his lecture. "This is the second school you've attended and the last one I will be paying for. If you think you will be transferring again—"

"I don't need to transfer, Dad. I told you I just got into SRB, and they made me a social chair." I huff hiking back up the hill, the sun beating down bringing sweat to the back of my neck. It's November, but the hottest time of day in Colorado still reaches the mid-seventies sometimes.

"Is that supposed to impress me, boy?"

I don't respond, because everything I want to say to my father, begins with fuck and ends with you, and that wouldn't go over well at Thanksgiving dinner in a few weeks.

"I called because Jinny is coming to do a school tour over winter break and I wasn't sure if you had classes and would be there?" he says, each word sounding genuine but lacking all care.

My cousin Jinny, a senior in high school, is absolutely thrilled to be coming to Conifer Valley next fall. So thrilled, in fact, that she got early acceptance. She tries to be here whenever she gets the chance. None of this is revolutionary information to me— Jinny and I are in constant communication. She's more of a sister to me than a cousin and honestly one of my closest friends.

"I will be here," I say, before I hear the line go dead.

"Love you too, Dad." I snark, as I shove my phone back into my pocket. I make it to the library doors just as a flutter of female students in basketball uniforms funnel out. I smirk, catching a few admiring looks as I hold the door open for them.

The air inside isn't too hot or cold. In Colorado the heater often turns on inside too early in the season, but today seems to be fine. The AC isn't blowing either though, so I trekked up the stairs to the second floor in hopes of finding cooler air.

Winding through the tables until I find my favorite chair that faces the window overlooking the mountain range, I pull out the paper back book that I have rolled into the back pocket of my black jeans and sit down to dive into it for the fourth time.

Promising myself that once I finish reading it, I will jump back up and find a solution to my issues, but until then I want to be just a normal human being— reading a book in silence.

Chapter Three

Wednesday

ELLE

T he soft buzz of the fluorescent lights slows as I dim the switch in the expansive meeting room. Luckily this semester I was able to book the nicest conference room in the main building on campus for our executive board meetings. Adorned with lush leather spinning chairs and a deep oak table surrounded by four flat screen televisions on each wall, for maximum presentation quality.

Every Wednesday at exactly 5:30 pm I waltz in to find my Vice President, Laura Everest, laying out agendas in front of each chair. Her silky black hair falling in waves across her sharp features. The soft pink off the shoulder sweater perfectly matching the warm undertones of her brown skin and deep brown eyes.

"I wasn't sure what setting you liked it at," she hums, as she flutters around the table to the thermostat. Her tight brown suede mini skirt and more fashionable than practical sweater reminds me that I should definitely reiterate to everyone the dress length requirements for formal meetings. Not that she's in violation of anything now, it's just members have been reporting each other left and right to the judicial board— regarding whether or not taller members need to have different criterias because their fingertips reach a high portion of their thigh, making it out of the bounds of the three finger width rule— so a formal announcement was well overdue.

"I don't mind," I say before sitting in the same chair I always do, to the left of Laura's— who sits at the head of the table in this circumstance.

Our Advisor, Leah, flutters through the door. Her long white tipped nails grip tightly around her phone as she murmurs into the tiny speaker from a distance. Reminding me that I also need to bring up nail polish colors for recruitment in the Spring. I write the note into my agenda, so I won't forget it. Followed by the word skirts, and for good measure I add a few more topics I want to mention.

Leah is a recent graduate from another university and a KSI alumni, getting her second degree in higher education through Conifer Valley's Master's School. Her history as her own chapter's president— and the fact that she seemed to have contacts at Brimham— granted her selection to become the advisor above all the other candidates that applied to KSI headquarters.

Everyone else would arrive a few minutes before six, most likely in a swarm of gossip. Until then the three of us would share the space, preparing for the weekly executive board meeting. I further settle into the cool leather seat, removing my black winter jacket and wrapping it around the back of my seat. Snow started to fall in the parking lot before I came in, so I threw it on just in case it was below freezing when the meeting ended.

Leah finally laughs and hangs up her call, finding my eyes immediately as she drops into the seat across from me— bracketing in Laura on either side. Laura keeps her brown eyes down, reviewing all the agenda points for the meeting, while Leah leans in to ask the same question she always does.

"How's it going?" she smiles, her bright white grin stretching her olive skin.

It is such a simple question, and a predictable one, but I never know how to answer. So I begin listing the things I learned from each of my meetings.

"Trent proposed another life altering idea in the president's council, and Holden is impressed by our service hours at the food bank."

"He would be, that man loves his community service." Leah's smile turns into a cheeky smirk, while tapping her forefinger on the wooden tabletop as she reviews the agenda quickly.

"Also," I hesitate because I know exactly how the next exchanges will go, "Lacy quit."

Leah clicks her tongue, and Laura's deep brown eyes fly up to meet mine.

"She didn't tell me anything," Laura huffs, "when did this happen?" Concern ruffles her soft angled brows together.

"She's been emailing me. Threatening to do it for weeks, but finally texted me today." I pull out my phone, opening it to the text exchange, before sliding it across the table to show them.

"Lacy's a great girl. Super friendly, but not really into holding a position." Leah states like she knew this was going to happen the second Lacy had been elected at the end of last semester.

"We have a social event in two weeks with SRB. What are we gonna do?" Laura says, checking her paper calendar and scribbling notes on her agenda before standing to collect the rest— presumably— to write in the change.

Lacy had managed to do something right, she had let me know before today's meeting, which meant it could be discussed in time to be added to the agenda for the chapter meeting on Sunday. Everything had to be introduced in advance. So that no one felt blind sided in front of the entire chapter in the formal meetings— when topics would be slated to vote on. Formal meetings followed a mix of secret rituals and Robert's Rule of Order. So the Executive board meeting being held in twenty minutes would also be held in Robert's Rule of Order.

Laura— like myself— hates when things change at the last minute, so I feel a bit sorry for not texting her earlier, but I had been rushing to get back to campus. After class I only had an hour or so to run home for dinner and to feed my cat Hubert before I had to be back. Some weeks I barely managed that. A quick basket of fries in the campus bar called Mile's— conveniently located next to this conference room— was often considered my dinner. The bar was named after the school's mascot, Mile's the Moose. Not my first choice for a name, or palace to eat.

Tonight it was the bagged salad from the local grocery store, quickly poured in the bowl and shoveled down, while I answered more emails and updated my digital calendar.

Shannon, the chapter's Judicial Chairman, enters with a brief nod of her black bobbed head before folding into her chair next to Leah. Mary and Minnie the twins that hold positions as the Recruitment Chair (Mary) and Scribe and Diversity Chair (Minnie) funnel in quickly after that. Hoisting their matching folded silver laptops up as they gossiped. Flipping their matching blond hair— only differentiated by the neon dyed tips, Minnie with pink ends and Mary with purple ones. Sipping on their matching jumbo cups— from the local coffee shop Smartboost. Clanking with ice and bright pink liquid sloshing around loudly.

"Hi," they sing in unison before tucking themselves into their designated spots.

"What happened to your eye?" askes Minnie.

Everyone turns to face me now, and a blush creeps up my cheek under their attention.

"I—" I hesitate, unsure what to say.

"You finally fight the Zeta Phi's president?" asks Francesca as she glides into the room flicking her long auburn ponytail around her torso. She's wearing a black mini skirt and red leather jacket— and never misses a beat, "You know, as Risk and Safety chair, I can't condone that, but as your best friend, I'm pissed I didn't get the video."

"I didn't punch Alicia, and you all know it would never happen." All eyes fixate on me, but no one smiles. I know that everyone always finds me intimidating— no matter what I say or how it's meant to come across— so I often add a parting remark. "We all know, I'd win anyways."

The murmur of laughter fills the space, as the remaining four members of the board flutter in a few minutes before the start. Lily (Bursar), Hillary (Panhellenic Delegate), Dakota (Academic Excellence Chair), and Sara (New Member and Sisterhood Development Chair) all find their spots around the table and prepare their folders or computers in front of them. Leah's gaze catches me as I face forwards again in preparation for Laura to call the meeting to a start.

"What?" I whisper.

"Oh nothing." She smirks, knowingly, before Laura clears her throat to settle all the groups chattering.

The meeting starts seamlessly, as always when Laura is in charge, so I am able to take a few notes for myself. But when the time comes to bring up Trent's idea, I hesitate. I don't personally think the school will give us an all Greek space, instead that it will inevitably bring to light all the negatives that the fraternities are doing. The University often keeps an eye on them, but they haven't asked for much in recent years. Trent is very ambitious so this will most likely be one of a long string of things that will be brought up to the Universities Board of Directors to review.

I want to make sure that my board members understand what it means to allow for another space, the amount of time and dedication to creating proposals would be. All while working with Trent, to make this happen. Which sounds like added hell to me, but mostly because I want to have a greater impact in my time as president. I don't want to simply have my name stamped next to all the rest in my short list of accomplishments. I want my own thing to boast about, it's just that I haven't come up with it yet.

So I brought up the proposal— reading from the sheet Holden had given us— and I watch them, checking in every few words. Watching their faces analyze every word of what I have to say, until I finally finish speaking.

"Isn't that what the Student Life Office is for?" asks Lily, clearly letting her cogs under her dark head of hair work over the numbers.

"Yes, but he wants a Greek-only space." I say.

"That doesn't seem very inclusive," chimes Minnie.

"Whose paying for all this?" Lily askes, clearly as unsure about the idea as I am.

"Trent didn't mention it."

"Well if he's asking for chapter funds, we don't have it," says Lily.

"It wouldn't be for a while though, right Elle?" asks Hillary, her soft undertone features are nicely painted with pink blush and matching eyeshadow. Everything about her screaming Barbie, from the bright blonde hair to the porcelain skin.

"We have a few months to decide, I think Holden is bringing it up at the beginning of the new year." I say, trying to sound impartial. I'm not allowed to boast my opinion, until it comes down to a tie breaking vote, so I can't let my disdain show.

"I think we should get more information before we bring it to the chapter, Trent obviously needs to ask them, because he hasn't thought about how it affects all of us." says Lily, narrowing her deep set eyes and typing away on her computer. Murmurs of agreement flutter from the rest of the group.

Laura was close to finishing up the meeting with closing remarks when she circles back to the topic of the social chair vacancy.

She doesn't slash Lacy in her speech, or make any ill remarks, she is clear and I admired her approach to the issue.

Until I hear her suggestion.

"And since our lovely president was social chair last year, I think she can handle the upcoming social event, and until we can vote on the chair for next semester."

"What?" I sit up straighter, hoping I heard her incorrectly.

Everyone seems more than thrilled at the suggestion and Leah beams brightly.

"I was a horrible social chair," I manage to say. Even though my heart is jackhammering.

"Oh hush you," Leah laughs. "You could use some positive socializing with the other Greek members. All you ever do is sit in meetings with them, I bet you hardly know anyone other than the presidents."

"That's not true." I crinkle my nose. "I know–"

"Yeah, name one other fraternity man in SRB, bestie," Francesca hollers from the far end of the room. She has her red leather sleeved elbows on the table as she watches me struggle— it's one of her favorite pastime activities.

"Um, Devin." I say, surprising even myself.

"Who's that?" Dakota asks, her thin lips in a tight line.

"Oh the new social chair!" Mary slaps Minnie's upper arm in excitement. "The hot one."

Something burns behind my heart at the thought of Mary or Minnie finding Devin attractive.

"The one that just transferred in?" asks Laura.

Astonished that Laura is gossiping along with them, I turn to face her. "I can't do this," I plead with her.

"Sounds like you're perfect for the job actually, since you and Devin are such good friends." Leah smiles.

I bit my lip at the suggestion while the others began discussing other members of Greek life that they find physically glorified.

"Alright," Laura states firmly, "we have come to a close, we all know our tasks for the next week and don't forget to send me updated reports for the formal meeting agenda. Thank you all, now go. The school closes in thirty minutes."

Everyone dashes from the room, excited to get out.

Everyone, except me, is most likely ready to head downtown for the night.

"Ladies night?" asks Francesca, as I collect my many folders and shove them into my bag.

"No, I have homework tonight." I say, clearly failing to hide my lie because Francesca just scoffs.

"So what big communications assignment do you have this week, deterring you from going to ladies night at Silver Spurs with us?" she asks as we make our way out into the hall, waving to Leah and Laura as they stay to have a private discussion. I normally would have stayed but I could tell Laura felt a bit overwhelmed by the sudden change in social chair status.

All the executive council chairs were to report to her, not me. But as Vice she struggles just as much as I do with making connections with some of the members. Most of them often chose one of the board members to disclose information to and it typically wasn't either of us, but alas Lacy chose me over Laura, and that probably stung.

"Maybe next week." I huff, pulling my tote bag higher on my shoulder.

"You really are going to break yourself carrying around that heavy thing all the time."

Francesca's auburn ponytail swishes behind her as she carries her single piece of paper and pen out of the meeting.

"I need all this stuff."

"All. The. Time." She drags each word dramatically.

"Yes–" I began, but she whirls in front of me, gripping my shoulders.

"What really happened to your eye?" she bends down to meet my gaze. We are the same height typically but she was wearing two inch bright red riding boots. She doesn't ride horses— just to be clear— but line dancing at the Silver Spur makes all the girls in Conifer Valley want to wear them. I also owned a pair, but they were from the days actually riding my horse back in Minnesota. She most likely is headed right to Silver Spur with Hillary. The two of them are practically inseparable, because they shared a townhouse off campus. Often the two of them host girls wine nights to watch trashy reality TV shows on a weekly basis.

"Devin ran into me."

"Devin?" Francesca's olive eyes light up at the sound of a boy's name out of my mouth, "Oh my god! You like him."

"I don't," I insist, pushing past her and striding past the front entry desk. Waving to Mel, the kind student who sits behind it every Wednesday evening.

"Okay well I'll believe you if you come out tonight." Francesca's angelic voice follows us out the double doors and into the parking lot.

"It's snowing." I state, wanting to change the subject.

"So, it's always snowing after homecoming." Francesca follows me to my small black SUV.

"Aren't you going to be cold?"

"NO," she dramatises, "because we never wait in line."

"Really?"

"Yeah, the bouncers know us, so we hardly have to wait. And even if it's the ones that don't, they don't like a bunch of girls in skirts shivering, so they take pity on us."

"Nice." I say, unlocking the door and leaning in to start the car. Our breaths start to form in front of us as we stare at one another a beat too long. "I'm not twenty one yet."

"So," Francesca huffs like it isn't an issue at all, "they'll just give you a stamp on your hand, but I know how to rub it off once we're inside."

"I really should study," I state, apprehensively, but want to appease my friend. I never "went out" because no one typically asked me to. Other than Frankie, no one asked me to do anything. Even when she did, the energy it took to stay up late was heavy to think about, but today I feel a bit lighter for some reason. My mundane was already interrupted by Devin, and the idea that I actually contributed to the sorority gossip for once was a bit exhilarating.

A horn honks from a small yellow car across the rows of empty spots, while flashing its headlights. It becomes clear that it's Hillary, her golden hair glowing in the cab, beckoning Francesca to hurry.

"Fine," I finally say, "just this once."

Squeals and hugs are exchanged, before she flutters away from me, skipping in her red boots as snow dances around her free spirit.

"We'll pick you up in an hour!"

"Hey Frankie," I yell, before ducking into my car's cab, "what do I wear?"

"SOMETHING HOT!" she screams, before diving into Hillary's awaiting vehicle.

———— ♦ ————

Something hot. *Something hot.*

I chant in my head as I tear through my tiny apartment closet. I own nothing that is considered hot, or even warm.

All my clothes consist of tee shirts, jeans, and an array of combat boots or sneakers. Even today, I am sporting my favorite green KSI stitched letters and deep navy jeans. I definitely couldn't wear letters to go out drinking. I quickly pull it over my head and throw it into my laundry bin, hoping removing the label will help me get into the mindset of drinking. Not that I was going to be underage drinking. I was turning twenty one in a few days, but I wasn't someone who drank outside the confines of her own apartment. My preference being white wine, but I doubt that's what Frankie and our other sisters drink at the Silver Spur.

I had only heard tales of the Silver Spur from the other Greeks and people at school. All about the line dancing lessons that took place and then the swing dancing couples that twirl around. Frankie often boasts about being selected multiple times a night to be spun and spun around in her hot red heeled boots. I would never be that hot, or asked to dance. Everything about me shouts "boring" and "don't pick her".

I never got selected in school for anything before being elected into positions in the sorority. That was the amazing thing about the chapter I'd chosen, they also chose me. And I truly felt that way most of the time, especially when I met Frankie the first day of Recruitment, clapping loudly along with the sisters as we waited in line to enter the recruitment room.

Frankie was one of the first to be invited into KSI—of course because she's gorgeous and fun. My complete opposite, but Frankie had chosen me to call her best friend and I've felt honored everyday since. She had her hardships too, we bonded over separated parents and being the only daughters, our love for wines from Oregon, knowing they were gonna be "the next big thing", and our love for country music.

Everyone found Frankie infectious and, therefore, tolerated me. I knew it, so tonight was becoming more daunting with every passing minute. Black sweaters and shiny shirts I had purchased for senior photos years were the only things that I considered.

A knock sounds at the door, and I quickly check the time. "Damnit, the only time you're early." I mutter while striding to open the door in my flimsy bralette and dark navy skinny jeans.

"Oh," a masculine voice startles me, as I open the door wider.

"Nate!" I exclaim, pulling a fluffy fur lined jacket off the hook near the door, and throwing my arms into the holes quickly. "What's up?"

"Sorry Elle, I just wanted to see if you had the notes from our Leadership Issues course."

Nate's dark brown eyes trace my body briefly before he notices me staring. He taps his bare feet along the carpet in the hall and I notice his sweatshirt sporting Colorado's NHL team across the chest.

"Yeah one second," I shuffle my socks across the laminate floor— back to my bag in the small living room. I flip through the pile that has formed, before gripping the small page of notes. "Hopefully you guys can get McRuffin back before next week's game, I saw his hit last game. It looked like he broke a collarbone."

"Yeah he did," Nate's voice brightens at the talk of hockey, "he's already been seen at the practice rink, so I'm hopeful." He doesn't expand on the topic further.

"Cool," I throw over my shoulder, unsure what else to say. It was the only thing I could think of at the moment, since it isn't *my* team.

"Are you going out?" Nate asks, still firmly planted in the hallway.

"Uh," I shuffle back to the door, "yeah I guess."

"Silver Spurs or Lasso's?"

"Silver Spurs." I give him a tight lipped smile, before handing him the single page of scribbles. "I didn't write very much down, not sure what help it'll be."

"Cool, my friends and I are going to Lassos on Friday."

"Oh nice," I say, gripping the door.

"Yeah." Nate says, with a tired smile, "maybe I'll see you there."

My phone begins to buzz on the counter, forcing me to finally break our eye contact. "Yeah, maybe!" I try to sound optimistic as I hike my thumb over my shoulder towards the kitchen.

"Bye, Elle."

"Bye, Nate." I shut the door and scramble to press the button before the call ends.

Francesca's alcohol soaked voice purrs on the other end, "change of plans Ellie! We will be at your place in five!"

"What?" I scramble to ask, raking my eyes over my dirty apartment, "like you're coming in?"

"Yeah, yeah we can come in if you want."

"No—"

"She said come on up guys!" Frankie's voice sounds far from the microphone.

"Does she have any alcohol?" a small voice— that sounds like Minnie— clambers from the far back of the phone line.

"Is that Minnie?"

"No Mary," Frankie slurs, "she's onlys drinks wines."

"I have wine," I say, optimistically.

"I know, I was telling Minnie, or never mind. Be there soon." The line ends before I respond.

"Fuck," I whisper, frantically throwing a few dishes into the cabinet and folding the drying mat up before tucking it under the sink. Then rushing to clean up my piles of papers on my coffee table.

Chapter Four

Wednesday

DEVIN

The second townhouse on the row of four, making up the "Le Cougar Trap"— as Trent has named it— smells like vomit and stale beer. Come to think of it, those two things didn't smell that dissimilar in a Frat house. He offered me a room in this shit hole when I first moved back to Colorado, at the start of the semester. I gave it a few days to "muddle over", at least that's what I told him. When actually I knew immediately. Only pretending to think about it as I unpacked the one box of things I owned into my "singles" on campus apartment. I hadn't brought much with me from California, so moving into my private dorm room on campus was easy.

My father made it seem like that would be the best option for me, so I wouldn't get distracted or focus on the dramas with any roommates. Which had bit me in the ass prior, but I didn't complain because the quiet was nice. Doing what my dad suggested always ended up being the best way to avoid any of his outbursts. I liked having my space to escape everything. But the longer I sat there, the more agitated I grew with Lacy, for leaving me to plan this social alone.

Trent would find out soon, if he hadn't already. That Lacy had quit, and I needed to have a plan for when he asked me what to do. So I thought, why not ask our Vice President, Seth.

Seth was the polar opposite of Trent, but still an ideal SRB brother. I liked Seth because he played kick around soccer on the weekends and had invited me multiple times. Knowing that I wanted to be on the university's team, but couldn't quite work up the nerve to try out.

Unfortunately for me, Seth lived in the same townhouse on "Le Cougar Trap" row that Trent did. The place was clean of debris, for now, but the scent embedded into the carpet was revolting. There was always a stream of people flooding in and out of the front door, especially the last four nights leading into the weekend, but I wasn't there for the mid-week party.

A swarm of cheers sounds from the living room, so I decide checking there will be first on the list. Another clammer of cheers and round of high fives is exchanged as the football team on the screen scores a touchdown. RJ and a few other Sigma Rho Beta brothers began chanting the receivers name and tossing a large brown football amongst themselves. I catch RJ's blue eyes first and he hurdles over the couch to give me a grip-fisted hug before performing the SRB secret handshake.

"Gotta practice the shake, little bro." He gruffs in my ear, as he slaps my shoulder with a firm palm, before throwing me back. His large linebacker frame only increases with all the beer and chili cheese fries he eats on a daily basis. His shaggy brown hair falls in locks over his brow. The handshake he was referring to isn't hard to remember, but he insists as my "Big Brother"— as fraternities call them— to make sure I remembered everything from my initiation.

Big Brothers were just that, a person in the chapter you could turn to for advice about girls or school— not that I needed help on either of those fronts, but having the instant friend was appreciated, especially because I was still learning all of the other brothers' names.

"Brooks and I were just about to toss the ball around," RJ says, forming a triangle with his thumbs in anticipation for the ball to come to him. "Wanna join?"

The ball slaps his palms as he catches it in a perfect spiral. I am still unsure which of the two dark haired men is Brooks. One of them was definitely named Geoff, I remembered because the name was pronounced "Jeff" and I was intrigued by that. Now staring at them both, they look too similar— especially in the matching red and gold football jerseys they now sported— to differentiate them.

"Uh, no." I try to not sound too harsh with my rejection. I don't like upsetting people. I often had to try really hard not to say everything I am thinking, if anything at all, because my tone is very monosyllable. "Sorry bro, I'm looking for Seth."

"Not here. But Trent's out back," RJ runs around the living room, pretending to juke the coffee table before diving onto the couch was a huge crack. Moans from Geoff follow. Or was that Brooks.

Unsure, I shake my head and duck outside onto the fragile— and very weathered— wood deck. The rust colored paint is starting to flake and I'm reminded how often my dad made me powerwash my childhood one in the summers. I ignore the itch to fix it and continue down the few steps into the patchy grass yard, where Trent and a few other brothers are setting up a folding table. As I inch closer the gravel mixes with the stray blades of brown lawn. Rocks and leaves crutch and Trent's brown eyes find me immediately.

"Devin! Great, you can help us set up the die table." Trent smiles a toothy grin.

"The what?" I find myself out of the loop again. Everyday in the Fraternity it seems something was hyphenated, or budding as a deep secret being to be revealed.

"It's this new game all the frats are playing out east." He brushes his hand over the colorful table top, fresh paint etches the letters SRB in navy letters. "They call it Snappa."

"Cool." I spit out, completely unsure why I had learned how to play flip cup last weekend if we were going to be learning new games each week. "I need to chat."

"What about?" Trent steers us away from the table now that four other brothers are standing at each corner. One of them tosses a die high into the air, then lets it hit the table with a loud snap.

"Lacy quit." I don't want to beat around the bush with this.

"I know." Trent sticks two fingers in his mouth and lets out an ear piercing whistle, before waving at the brothers hauling in a pair of kegs through the pickett french gate. "Those go in the ice coolers on the deck, not the grass."

My ears ring for a brief moment, then I hear Trent whisper, "imbécile," before turning to me again.

"What am I supposed to do if they don't have a chair for me to work with?"

"Look," Trent grips my shoulder. He seems to do that alot. "Just plan the thing, I know it's your first or whatever, so it won't matter. Then when the KSI's get their shit together they'll just show up, you know."

I nod along with him, before realizing that none of what he says is helpful, "wait no."

"Mec," Trent says, throwing his perfectly styled head back in exaggeration, "you need to chill. None of it matters, we will just go bowling like you said. There. It's planned, now let's get a drink."

Trent doesn't wait for me to follow him, or to respond. To him it is that simple— just another Wednesday evening. His house was beginning to fill with patrons, and he had issues more tedious than mine. I let out an exasperated breath before tucking my hands in my front pockets. The air starts to cool and a few flutters of snow kiss my skin. By sundown, the entire party will be inside and I would be cramped against a wall waiting for the perfect time to slip out of the house without Trent bothering me for pulling an Irish goodbye again.

As I make my way into the kitchen I notice a few brothers standing at the front door, like bouncers of sorts, checking out the few women who have just arrived. Making them spin while they smile wildly in their short skirts and crop tops. It is shocking how little clothes the women in Colorado wear, similar to California— and don't get me wrong I love it— but the freezing nights are a bit scarier for them to be wearing such little protection from the cold.

The scent of weed floods my nostrils and I follow it to the back bedroom, only to find a group of men and women sitting around passing a bong. I recognize the scrawny kid in all army green, Garret— another SRB brother. I nod at him when he directs his bloodshot eyes my way.

"Bathroom?" I ask, in an attempt to redirect my lost nature.

"Yeah, next left." He says, before taking the bong from a small girl sporting braids who looks about the age of Jinny.

How am I supposed to protect Jinny from all of this, she will be so amused by boys like Trent that she would definitely end up here. Next year I will be like an overbearing father following her around.

The bathroom smells worse than the rest of the house, so I quickly take a piss. There isn't even any hand soap for the women to use. I look under the sink to find a pile of toilet paper rolls and an old wrench but nothing to place out for them, so I leave.

Back out into the hall, I have to shift a few times to squeeze past a few groups of girls as they giggle and flick their eyes over my towering form. Every fiber of my being urging me to get outside and away from the musty townhouse, as it packs full with people. Until a small voice stops me in my tracks.

"Yeah, and I heard the *Ice queen* actually went out tonight."

"Truly?" Laughs bubble out from another girl, across from the first who spoke.

"They went to the Silver Spur because they aren't allowed at SRB house parties anymore." They continued to speak about a mile a minute and then a third girl chimes in, before handing them all red plastic cups filled with bright blue liquid.

"You know she gave the ELN president the golden Cougar that Trent had over the mantle last spring. Just went up. Took it down, and handed it over."

"Wow no wonder Trent hates her."

I watched bemused, unsure when to interject, because they spoke at the speed of light. I hardly pieced together that ELN meant Epsilon Lambda Nu— our rival Fraternity— but the idea of learning more about Elle itched me deeply. I was able to forget about her for a few hours, but her image still burned into my brain. I wanted to blame it on the fact that I had assaulted her and I felt bad about that. Which I did, but I was also a bit stung by her rejection and addicted to the look in her eyes when I called her out for lying. She was like a surprise gift on Christmas.

I didn't know I wanted it until I started opening it and peeling back the layers of flimsy wrapping that held the box so uptight.

"Are you all in KSI?" I ask, not knowing any other approach into the gossip mongers circle.

It was an obvious mistake as the look of disgust washes across their faces, before the first girl, a petite blonde wearing too much eyeshadow says, "Ew, no. We're Zeta Phi's."

All of their faces are now a mix of pinched noses, crinkled brows, and shadowy eyelids. One even snarls as she gives me a once over that makes me feel like I was wearing nothing but my boxer briefs.

I can fix this, girls are easy to impress.

So I flash my teeth and cross my arms over my chest to flex my biceps in front of them. "Of course you beautiful ladies are, I was only joking." They seem to relax at this statement, but still don't say anything else, so I continued, "I'm a new SRB brother, and I have never heard that story before, can you tell it again."

Girls love to gossip, especially sorority sisters.

Within one breath the blonde girl starts her very long story again, "Elle was the one who handed over the golden cougar that Trent had bought for the house, right after they moved in to the president of the other frat. She was

all drunk and playing pong with them but when Jack—
the president before Stephan— snuck in. She just like
handed it to him. I saw the whole thing, she acted like she
didn't know who Zach was, even though she was like KSI's
social chair or whatever. She just laughed and continued
playing the game, until Trent found out. Because he was
also president at the time. You know he's like a two time
elect right?"

Her hands fly around and another breath is taken, but
she doesn't stop talking.

"Anyways, Trent stormed in and kicked her and the rest
of the KSI out of the townhouse and placed a ban on all
of them. So they aren't allowed at his parties anymore,
basically."

I don't know what to say, so I wait for her to finish
speaking.

"Now they all go to that trash bar, Silver Spurs, on
Wednesdays because it's like eighteen and up at night or
whatever, and they can all get in. It's like fun on Saturday
nights but Lasso's has way hotter men that like to wear
cowboy hats and know how to dance."

"Wait, Elle went to Silver Spurs tonight?" I manage to
get in before the girls continue gossiping.

"Yeah, I got a Zapchat from Chris saying Frankie was
there."

"Can I see?"

"NO." The look she throws at me, is similar to one given to a person who has just discovered alien life, for not knowing how Zapchat worked. "It was only a few seconds long, but I can check Frankie's story, I follow her too." She rolls her eyes and pulls her phone out of her knee high boot, "Alright here." She says, thrusting the small video into my view.

A grainy video of a girl with scarlet red hair, spinning around a wooden dance floor, flashes along the screen. Nothing seems to be happening other than her filming herself screaming along to a Luke Bryan song, but then a flash of brown hair catches my eye.

Elle is being spun around the dance floor by a man in a black cowboy hat. He looks to be my dads age. He is gripping her slender waist with tight hands, and my knuckles turn white as I crush the phone in my tight grasp.

Her dark skinny jeans, the same ones she was wearing earlier that day, hug her ass tighter than the man's hands are and for some damn reason my heart rate picks up at the thought of her being touched by anyone. What if she was getting even more attention by explaining to them about how the black eye she sported was from a man, "that I had hit her". She would be getting drinks, and more, from any man who would be telling her that *that man* was a pig, that *I was a pig*. She would be laughing and agreeing with them, making it more believable in her head that I had hit her intentionally.

The phone flashes back to a white list of names and emojis. The blonde pulls her phone from my fingers and turns her friends away from my wild gaze, I don't care what they think. I need to get out of this damn house. Because Elle was out there with men and letting them touch her, and for some damn reason everything in me wants to stop that. Wants to be the owner of the hands touching her.

I scramble out the door and find a group of brothers giving a few girls piggy back rides, as they head towards a truck parked on the street. Recognizing one of them as Geoff, or Brooks. Unsure I just began shouting after them. Luckily, one is Geoff and turns immediately.

"Where are y'all headed?" I ask, hoping it is on the way to Silver Spur.

"We're headed to Lasso's"

That isn't going to work I think, but instead I say the first thing I think Trent would in this situation, "What about Silver Spur, it's eighteen and up tonight."

I'm not proud of the approach, mostly because the two guys just roll their eyes at me. As the girls squeal excitedly, chanting "Yes, yes, yes, Silver Spur. Silver Spur."

"Alright," moans Geoff, placing the girl on his back onto the black pavement before climbing into the driver's seat, "Let's go."

I hop into the cab next to the women and ignore them as they try to introduce themselves. I drowned them out with my thoughts. I was headed to the Silver Spur, and the only girl I cared about was Elle.

Chapter Five

Wednesday

ELLE

"Just order a vodka soda."

"Absolutely not." I seeth, hoping no one can hear us. The crowd around the bar is filled with men I don't recognize and sorority sisters that I do. I definitely wasn't going to be seen drinking in front of them, when they all know I am underage.

"Come on, your birthday is on Tuesday. That's like tomorrow."

"Actually it's a week away from yesterday, technically."

"Stop being so technical!" Frankie shouts at me, before she takes a sip from the small straw sticking out of her Vegas Bomb, "you just had wine at your place."

"What can I get you?" the bartender appears in front of me, her tight bra of a shirt pushing her boobs up to her chin.

"Water?" I say, sheepishly.

"It's down there." She points to the other end of the bar, to a jug with a tiny stack of plastic cups piled next to it, before strutting away a bit annoyed I wasn't a paying customer.

"Come with me to the bathroom," Frankie tugs on my wrist as I eye the water jug— shrinking the further we walk from it.

"I need water," I interject, realizing my mouth was getting very dry in the hot bar. I only danced with one man, and I stepped on his toes so many times he switched me out for Frankie before the song even ended.

"Drink from the sink," Frankie throws over her shoulder, as she grabs Hillary and instructs her it is time for everyone to, apparently, use the bathroom together.

"Um, no," I say, absolutely repulsed by drinking tap water. Not that Colorado water isn't healthy to drink. I personally have just seen too many documentaries about the heavy metals and their effects they have on our skin. We are what we put into our bodies. Which is why I also didn't eat meat and only buy organic produce. My one exception to that rule is alcohol, of course, and the french fries from Mile's. I pretend that the University buys organic potatoes, so it is easier to eat them.

The girls bathroom is an array of pink wallpaper with pinup cartoons of cowgirls flashing their asses and spinning lassos. Naked plastic dolls have been nailed to the trim closest to the ceiling, which decorates the highest part of all the walls. It smells like a mixture of perfumes and a bit of vomit. Which is explained once we hear the girl in the first stall wrenching, as her friend stands holding the door to the stall shut. Reminding her friend that "it's going to be alright."

The entire mirrored wall above the counter of sinks is filled with faces applying lipstick or adjusting flyaway strands of hair. A group of girls a few years older than us squeals when Frankie enters, hugging her and bringing her closer for a mirror selfie, before fussing over her like mother hens.

I slip into the stall that has just become vacant and listen to the giggles as I pee quickly. Twisting my dirty boots on the sticky floor. They have been through alot on the farm back home, but this sticky floor is the first and hopefully the last they'll be stuck to.

As I emerge to wash my hands and fix my hair, Frankie and Hillary wave goodbye to the girls before hopping up to sit on the edge of the counter, their backs pressed into the corner. I reach for the roll of paper, next to them. Disgusted that it isn't inside the black compartment that it's meant to be held in. I rip off a small piece then toss it into the can that hangs in the wall when I'm done. It bounces off, and hits the growing pile that overflows into a mass of many crumpled sheets on the floor.

Frankie and Hillary snap a bunch of photos before Frankie tugs my arm and I fall into her knees as she tucks my small face into the frame for a photo.

"I love that one!" Hillary exclaims as they review it. "What do you think?" She pushes the screen into my face. All I can see are two gorgeous women and plain old me, with a half opened eye on one side and a double chin where I thought my single one rested.

"Uh," I start, before Frankie jumps off the counter and strides for the door.

"We can take more later." Hillary says, obviously reading my expression.

I hang my head low as we exit the bathroom in a line, allowing more girls through in a zippered fashion. Most of them fan over Frankies boots or Hillary's shiny blonde hair.

"Do you know them?" I yell up to Hillary as we round the corner.

"No," she smiles for the first time at me, and I am stung by the fact that her rosy expression is pinned on *me*— out of all humans in this bar. She has a smile that makes you feel special, and matched with her shiny blonde hair and perfect teeth, it was a true surprise she is a KSI. Because everyone and school often said anyone who looked like her was in Zeta Phi Nu. Which most likely aided her success as our Panhellenic Delegate for the chapter. Her impartial friendly nature really helps us with sorority relations, especially during recruitments.

"That's just how it is in the girls restroom," she says, matter of factly.

As we make our way back to the dance floor a line of people begins to form, and a Kenny Chesney song— that plays on the radio everyday— starts to blare alive. I am dumb founded by the synchronization of all the dancers as they tap the toes, then heels, before they spin around, then flick their legs around with such grace. They continue the same steps facing the other direction now and the crowd's cheers grow wild.

Frankie pushes through the crowd, until she rests her hand on the rail that cages in the scene of line dancers. I became transfixed by all their boots making beautiful stomps to the music, the wood becoming a large drum. A pair of black and white sneakers stick out from the crowd and step to the row right in front of us. Black jeaned legs scattered with holes stomps along with the crowd as they all turn to continue the dance facing us. It is truly amazing that a person wearing sneakers— one's that I often like to wear— is brave enough to line dance along with all the flashy boots.

I knock a few half filled plastic cups to the floor when my eyes find the hazel pair attached to the man sporting said sneakers.

"Devin?" I squeak.

The devious grin that graces my presence only a matter of hours ago in Holden's office flashes at me, he continues the steps with perfect accuracy as his gaze traces my form. I need to pull my gaze away, but his dimple and glorious smile keeps me firmly locked in this stand still.

Finally the dancers turn, but he fakes to follow them, whipping his head back to me, while continuing the dance in the opposite direction of everyone else. Still perfectly synced with the line, so that when the group moves one direction, he does too.

His staring is making so much heat rise to my face, and he obviously is unaware of the awkwardness because when the song ends he starts right in my direction. Unsure what to do, I dive for the cups that have spilled to the floor, before stacking them and placing them on the small lip of the rail at the edge of the dance floor.

"Hello Your Highness," his deep voice says, and the sound of Luke Bryan's newest hit starts to play. His hair is messy, like he's been running his hands through it endlessly. Small parts of it stick to his glossy skin, while others bounce as he shifts his stance to lean towards me.

"Um, hi," is all I manage to push out, before noticing Hillary and Frankie wide eyed next to me. All the girls on the dance floor shake their hips to the song every time Luke asks them to shake it, but Devin just stands there. Towering over me, with his original height added on to the few inches that the dance floor garners him. He's wearing the same clothes he had been that morning, with no shame that he has sweat on his skin. He grips the rail with strong arms— flexing them further under his maroon tee shirt— as he leans close to my ear.

The whisper of his breath sends a shiver down my spine, and his voice manages to go even lower in octaves, "Dance with me?" The scent of pine tar body wash and rock star sex appeal wraps around me, and my eyelids flutter closed.

This is how we should have met the first time.

My mind races with the possibilities of me accepting the dance. Then a million reasons not to do so abruptly overlap the first ones.

"I don't know how to do that," I say, opening my eyelids quickly and pointing to the swarms of girls spinning around. The song ends and patrons start to clear out of the way, but Devin remains gapping at me with his wide smile.

"I know you can two-step, Elle." His dimple dances on his left cheek again as he smiles and holds out his hand. "Remember, I know everything."

He says it like a warning but his playful nature molds it into a droplet of hope that falls deep into the oceans of my subconscious.

"I–" I'm in shock— that's what was happening— somehow I went from the girl who never went out on a Wednesday night, to the one being asked to dance at a bar by a fraternity man. I'm not the girl who pines after those types of men, so I am smart enough to realize this shit only happens in movies.

Frankie shakes my shoulders, "Bitch, if you don't get in there...I will."

Her use of the word bitch was meant to be endearing but it only adds to the shock. I am not this girl, I am the president of Kappa Sigma Iota, not a partier. I'm an average grade obtainer, and vegetarian eater, not a risk taker or cowgirl line dancer. Devin is making me question all of that, as what if's fly into my head.

What if I danced? What if I liked it? What if I liked him?

I stomp all those thoughts down. Tonight, I could do this.

For tonight.

I did need to talk to him after this, and I could resist his allure. Be professional. He most likely did this to lots of girls, so I could be one of the many for tonight. My heart betrays me as that thought sinks in my gut.

"Okay," I say, turning to round the corner of the dance floor. Large hands grip my torso and my feet fly out from under me as Devin flings me over the railing and my brown boots hit the hardwood dance floor with a thud.

If I wasn't in shock before, I certainly am now. His hand rests under my arm, his fingertips grazing the strap of my bra through my thin fabric shirt. My breath catches in my chest. He isn't aware of this though as he leads us to an opening on the dance floor.

An entirely new song begins playing, but no time is allotted for me to consider my next move, Devin's hand moves to my hip and tugs me to meet his solid form with mine. His other hand clasps over my palm, hoisting it up in the air next to his shoulder. I look up at him to see his infamous smile and dimple blasted down at me. He starts to guide us and my feet fall into the groove. I trip slightly when he tries to turn us, but he doesn't stop. He only presses my chest tighter to his and lifts me gracefully off the ground.

"Let me lead, Your Highness." His hot breath tickles my ear again.

My shoulder blades sag and I let out a sigh of relief at the feeling of letting them relax. Devin is an excellent dancer, even though he wears the wrong shoes and sticks out in the crowd like a sore thumb. He doesn't seem to care or notice that fact at all, he just keeps his hazel eyes locked on mine. The lights are a soft umber glow and the disco ball over head bounces off small silver rays that flutter across his face.

I recognize the song as "More Hearts than Mine" by Ingrid Andress and I hope it isn't life playing a very sick game, because my heart starts to beat a bit faster as Devin spins me away from him. Then whips me back with such force I feel like I'am going to fall flat on my face. But he holds me firm, tucking his fingers through the loops in my jeans and clutching my sweaty palm like he's afraid to let me go.

He doesn't say anything else to me as the next song comes on, and it is worse than the previous. "Girl Crush" by Little Big Town pulls more couples onto the floor around us and I let my gaze fall to them, all slowing their pace and tucking their head into one another.

I'm in serious trouble. Because the man gripping me, as we continue dancing to the second song, is seeming a little too familiar for actually being the person who had almost broken my nose just this morning. A bit of a stretch, since I had worse hits playing recreation hockey growing up. But as I looked up I realized, I indeed, had *a crush* on the man in front of me.

What was worse than that, was the reminder that came in the forms of hoots and hollers from Frankie and Hillary when the song ended and I pulled away. The reality of the fact that Devin is a SRB— and that I had banned myself from any fraternity men— hip checks me.

I back away, unsure what to say or do, so I fucking embarasse myself further by bowing into a courtesy— like a real idiot— before fleeing from the dance floor. Gripping Frankie by the elbow, I pull us towards the bathroom again. Beginning to feel the appeal of its vomit scented sanctuary.

My gaze shoots back to find Devin gleaming like he has just won the Stanley Cup. His buddies clap onto his shoulders while handing him a plastic beer filled one. And like everything he did with such great sex appeal, he tosses the liquid down his throat without ever taking his hazel eyes off me.

Chapter Six

Thursday

DEVIN

I cy blue eyes are all I can think about, sitting above perfect pink lips that she keeps wetting with her tongue. No, that tongue is all I can think about. The sweet scent of her hair.

All I can think about is Elle.

"Alright guys!" Seth says in a way to close the meeting, "if you have any questions just text me."

I adjust my semi hard boner in my jeans before standing to leave the small conference room we have just spent the last hour in. It is the last place I want to be on a Thursday afternoon, but Trent insists that I attend the meeting if I want to be social chair. Which I do even more now that Elle was in charge of the position for the KSI chapter. Trent had texted me about the news after I had woken up from the best dream I had in years last night. Elle's perfect tongue tracing circles around the tip of my...

"Devin," Trent calls after me, interrupting my day dreaming, "hold back for a moment."

"Sure," I manage to choke out, before turning around and facing him and Seth, who still sits in the leather chairs that surround the dark wood table, "What's up?"

"Are you okay working with Elle for the social?" Seth shoots me a look indicating he is leading up to something larger.

"Yeah," I say, hesitantly, "why?"

"She can be a bit of a bitch," blurts Trent. My fists clench. "You know they don't call her the Ice Queen for nothing."

Holding my tongue locked in place as my teeth grind—I need to stay on Trent's good side. I knew how all this worked, organizations with leadership and I wouldn't be underestimating another leader if I could help it. I wasn't able to transfer again, if I wanted my dad to pay for my school I needed to fall in line as he instructed.

"I can manage." I finally huff, still standing. Hoping that was the extent of our conversation.

"Sit, Devin," Seth gestures to the chair I had vacated moments ago. Again because I am a good person and brother I do as he asks.

"Trent was hoping to ask you something else."

I wait for Trent to continue, cocking my head in his direction. He smiles a devious smile that I recognize immediately as the one that is hiding something awful.

"No." I say, without letting him start.

"You don't even know what I was going to say."

"I know that look," I say. "It's the same one you had when you asked me to trash the girls locker room with you for your senior prank." That prank had gotten us both directly to the principals office, and it wasn't even the best prank pulled that year by his fifty person class in our mountain town high school. Everyone knew it was Trent because he couldn't keep his pretentious mouth shut and I got dragged into everything bad like I always did. He got to graduate and I got detention the first week of my senior year.

"That was fun," he smiles, "and you know it."

"No." I stand, my chair catching on the floor and beginning to tip before I catch the back of it.

"It's not like that," Seth is throwing looks between Trent and I, "we need your help."

"With what?" I ask, impatiently.

"I need all the presidents to vote yes for the All Greek Space," Trent says. "Including the–"

"Don't call her that."

"I knew you'd be perfect for this," Trent smiles again, "I need her to vote yes."

"What do you expect me to do?"

"Were you not dancing with her all night at Silver Spur last night?" Seth says, attempting to add to their, seemingly obvious, intervention.

"We danced once." It was a lie, we danced for exactly six minutes and forty seven seconds, I made sure to count. Then double check the lengths of both the songs we danced to when I got back to my dorm room. "It's a free country."

"We aren't saying you can't dance with her," Seth adds with a small sigh, " We just know that you are friends now."

"And you need to convince her to vote yes," adds Trent, his smile was tight lipped but curved at the ends.

"How am I supposed to do that?"

Trent's smile opens and I know he's thinking of a dirty joke to add.

"Don't." I say, shooting him a scathing look.

He holds his hands, defensively, "just figure it out. I need her acceptance to get Holden on board."

"I doubt that." I roll my eyes. Trent is always trying to play a long game and he had been boasting about this proposal in the chapter meetings for the last few weeks, he also had no issue explaining that not all of the presidents were on board.

"It's my job to worry about that," Trent says as he stands, "I need you, Mec."

"Here." Seth slides a small yellow paper across the table towards me, a ten digit number is scribbled in his messy handwriting. "It's Elle's number."

I grip the note quicker than an unbiased man should and shove it into my front pocket, before turning around to exit. Intentionally before Trent.

I'm not fast enough because his long strides are next to mine before we reach the stairs that aim down to the main floor of the building.

"This is actually so perfect, you know the last KSI president dated a SRB and we were able to get so much done." Trent rambles on, and I take two steps at a time down the small dimly lit staircase before emerging at the base that leads to the campus bar. I didn't intend to head that way, but I need a beer and Trent will inevitably follow me around until he realizes he has somewhere more important to be. "I can't believe I didn't think of this sooner."

I hum in response, not trusting myself to form an actual response.

"What can I get you boys?" Asks the student behind the bar, his name tag labeling him a John and he looks as basic as the name states.

"Redbird Ale, please" I say, not wanting to sit around and ask questions. It is the only one I recognized, its burly white Yeti flying down a hill on disproportionate ski's, standing out amongst the other handles along the back wall. John tugs on it and golden amber liquid fizzes out of it briefly, before it sputters and spews mostly foam.

"Sorry, I gotta go fix the keg," John grumbles before shooting through the double swinging doors and disappearing from sight.

"How are you going to do it?"

"Do what," I finally manage to turn myself to face Trent, who is looking over the tiny plastic menu like he is going to stay and join me, and I really hope he doesn't.

John comes back and fiddles with the handle again, before pouring the perfect pint of amber ale, and sliding it across the bar. "Open or closed?"

"Closed," I say, sliding my card across the counter for him to swipe.

"How are you going to convince the Ic—"

I growl and turn towards Trent, swiping my card and shoving it back in my wallet before gripping my cold beer. I need to keep my hands busy before I do something I will regret.

"I mean Elle," Trent senses my anger, "how are you going to convince her?"

"I don't know."

"But you're going to, right?" he presses.

"Trent." I shuffle my feet towards the open table in front of the small stage, a group of students are fiddling with the sound machines and cords that lead to the microphones. "I don't really want to talk about this while I try and enjoy my beer."

"I'm just curious, Mec." Trent sits across from me, pulling out his phone and typing away endlessly. While I drive my upper lip through the foam on top of my beer and take a huge swallow of the slightly sour citrus liquid.

"What's the show tonight?" I ask the man fiddling with the extension cords. He is knelt close to our table along the front of the stage. I suck the foam stuck to my upper lip off with my bottom teeth.

"It's Thursday night Trivia," he says, then sets back to work— stretching and taping down all the loose cords in a neat line.

The yellow paper in my pocket is starting to burn— the need to pull it out and send a text driving me mad. I don't want to text her with Trent here. He would inevitably taint the entire experience. I would have rather her have given me her number willingly, but I can play this off. She was more than aware I am the social chair and even though we hadn't spoken much last night, I could tell she enjoyed dancing with me. She was quiet as I spun her around that wooden dance floor, but I caught the smile that peaked out a few times.

She is a very intriguing individual, and a smile tugged at my lips at the memory of her bowing to me before running away. Every fiber of my being had wanted to chase her but Geoff had told me the girls they brought were too drunk to stay, prompting us to leave. I didn't see her on the way out and I didn't say farewell, but I knew I'd see her again. It was a small University and a small Greek life, so we'd run into each other eventually. I selflessly wanted that day to be today.

"Alright," Trent says, abruptly, before throwing his phone back into his pocket. He stands and straightens his navy polo. He has a large collection of freshly pressed SRB embroidered polo shirts and rotates them often. "I'm out."

"Okay." I grumble, glad for him to leave me.

"I'm not asking you to get you in any trouble you know." He scolds, before striding for the door. That is the most he will say on the subject.

We never got into all the gritty details of my transfer, I simply told him I was forced out because I took the blame for something I didn't do, and he didn't push. Parts of me wished he had, because I had no one else to talk to about my previous issues. Another part of me was thankful I could leave it in the past. So I boarded up the topic in my mental box and shoved it under the metaphorical bed— much like the real one I used to hide the dirty magazines that my uncle gave me for my sixteenth birthday.

I pull out my phone and the yellow note with Elle's number on it. I type it into my contacts then hover over the name for a brief second. I want to add her as something other than Elle, mostly because she holds some weight in my chest already. The name doesn't seem to fit her as the person she is to me.

Who was she to me? Oh was I in for it.

I settle for something that will hold weight but won't be obvious to anyone if it popped up unexpectedly.

A small part of me hoped that one day I'd have a group of close buddies that would joke about my old lady calling. Most men my age didn't want that but when you've lost your mom at a young age like I had, having a wife to spend my days with was a very admirable goal in my eyes.

Not to say Elle would be that wife, but maybe...

I stop my mind before it spins out of control and start a new message. I can't add her number to it right away because I truly don't even know what to say.

"Hey it's Devin," doesn't seem like something that would stop traffic, let alone get her to respond.

"What's up? Heard you are helping plan the social," seems to direct, and all too laborious.

No, Elle is snarky, and would definitely like something she could snap back to. I just had to come up with something that didn't sound completely lame. I set the phone down on the table, rubbing my sweaty palms on my thighs before taking another large gulp of my beer.

What could I say?

I do need to see her, so we can talk about the social, but I don't want to talk to her about that. I want to know more about *her*, which gives me an idea. My fingers start flying across the screen then hover over the message briefly, before I hit send.

I wait for her to respond. Starting to feel dumb that I have been staring at my phone for so long, so I swipe it from the table and lock it.

Before throwing it back into my pocket.

I wait for it to buzz, thinking it does multiple times, but it's only an email from Trent about Sunday's meeting.

The second time it buzzes it's my dad calling, I silence it and tuck it back in my pocket. I toss back my beer and promptly leave Mile's before the trivia crowd funnels in.

Every face I pass, I search for Elle. Hoping I run into her. Wishing she'd text me back. I start to feel more anxious about it when I bound outside and aim down the large hill towards the dorms. The late fall chill that circles in the wind is biting my skin, but as I slip into the last building on the strip of student housing that pain doesn't even distract me from checking my phone.

Still nothing.

I check to see if she read the message, but it doesn't say.

The cold air in my room is no different from the chill outside, because I had left my window cracked. Slamming it shut I throw my phone on the nightstand, hoping it's broken. I plug it into the charger that lives forever attached to my wall outlet.

Nothing.

Maybe if I took a shower and walked away from it, it would buzz alive. So I force myself away from the device and into the ensuite bathroom, turning the shower to the hottest setting.

I stripe down naked and stare at my reflection.

"Be cool, Devin." I flex my anger into my shoulders and think about how I should hit the gym in the morning. Maybe Elle is a gym rat or whatever the girls call it. Maybe she'll be there bright and early. If she was anything like Trent, she'd be constantly busy.

I let out an exasperated breath. I need to get her out of my brain, so I hop in the shower. But with one bump on my semi-hard dick, the image of her floods in. So instead I fuck my hand until I pump the image of her right out of my head.

It doesn't work, because when I finally run the shower out of hot water, I'm flying across the room in my towel, almost tripping over the small sag carpet, at the sight of my phone buzzing alive. A huge shit eating grin touches my face as multiple text messages from Elle pop up in little bubbles on the screen.

Chapter Seven

Thursday

ELLE

I was so over the moon that Hillary had asked me to be in the meeting, that I didn't check my phone the entire time. Wanting to be the picture of professionalism, as I sat next to Alicia Hawkins (the president of Zeta Phi Nu), who had also been asked to attend along with Whitney, the president of Gamma Omega Rho. Turns out, all three chapters hadn't retained enough numbers during recruitment to make our campus quotas, so we were being asked to hold a joint Spring Recruitment next semester.

I briefly notice, for the first time, that I have an unread text message but it is from an unknown number. It isn't odd for me to get random messages, I have about sixty sorority sisters and about forty other Greek numbers already in my contacts. This isn't one of those, I actually was stumped by the message in particular, because the person obviously knows it is me, but I'm not getting any context clues to who it is.

Another message pops up from Frankie, saying she added me to a group called **Friday Night Girlies Group**— it also has about a hundred bright emojis in the title. I click on it but no other messages show until she messages again.

Frankie: I added Ellie.

Dani: Who?

Hillary: The Prez.

Dani: Oh shit

Frankie: Don't do that.

Keeping up with the messages proves to be difficult— by the time I make it to my car and start warming it up— about fifty other messages have already popped up. Discussing everything from outfits for Friday, to beverage choices, and if they are going to match their nails to their shoes. I don't know what to say, so I quickly swipe through them until I see a question directed at me from Hillary.

Hillary: Are you coming then Elle?

To what?

Frankie: She's joking lol

Dani: Can we still drink?

Frankie: Yes, don't ask stupid questions.

Hillary: She's joking. Yes, Elle drinks too. Right Elle?

Yeah

The warm air from my car turns scolding so I adjust the temperature and switch my phone to silent. I only had a few minutes worth of a drive to my student apartment down the large hill. I don't want to risk being distracted in this condition. Driving in Colorado isn't much different than in Minnesota, except for the people who still buy two wheel drive cars— for some odd reason. The snow is always looming from late October all the way to April some seasons, so having a car that couldn't handle the conditions seems silly to me.

The drive is uneventful, so when I pull into the garage and find my spot, I'm swept up to the elevators without ever having to think about my phone.

I fling the door open to Hubert's loud crying telling me he is starving. Which is a gross exaggeration, because he is the size of a small ottoman. Round and cuddly just like all the best tabby cats are. Student dorms did not allow for cats which is why I begged my mom to help me qualify for off campus student housing. It took an entire summer of filing her accounting paperwork at her office, but she let me log the hours as "internship work" for my resume. The extra hundred bucks a week helped too. To save, to pay for the sorority this semester, and my extra cost of living. I had a part time job in the summers as well, back home at the local indoor ice rink. Handing out skate rentals and picking up a few extra kids skates, which were fun because I just got to glide around all the small children instructing them to continue in a clockwise direction.

I pour a heap of food into a Hubert's bowl and flick the kettle on as I pass it to quickly change into a pair of black sweat-pants and my favorite green sweatshirt, sporting my favorite NHL team logo. I sweep back into the small beige galley kitchen and drop a bag of my favorite peppermint tea into my white porcelain mug, before filling the kettle back up with the filtered water jug in the fridge.

With my tea secured, I settle into the couch. Wrapping myself in my blanket, I pull my laptop and phone out of my bag before flipping open my screen and begin reviewing the emails I hadn't responded to yet. Messages began popping up rapidly in the corner reminding me to turn my phone off silent.

Immediately all the messages from the group chat ring in, I flick through them quickly before silencing the entire group with a single setting change. The other message from the unknown number also sits there. I open it and read it fully, still confused who sent it and how to respond.

ur all i can think about elle. when can i see you again?

No one's face is popping into my mind. Not a single soul from Greek life, or my classes, or even my old high school.

No one I knew would have sent that to a stranger, so I simply type out my first thought. Then send my second as well, a small bubble of hope growing as I watch dots form on the other end.

Who is this?

Also never if you don't tell me?

Unknown: what if i say please and promise to kiss the ground you walk on.

Why don't you say your name?

Unknown: hmmm... that's too easy.

So is reporting a stalker to campus security.

Unknown: okay your highness, damn, it's devin.

Oh.

Devin SRB: oh?

Devin SRB: that's all you have to say?

What do you want?

Devin SRB : to take you to dinner?

N.O.

Devin SRB: damn my heart is shattered again.

Sorry.

Devin SRB: you should be. ur the one that broke it when we met.

I think you're thinking of my nose.

Also why do you use proper punctuation but not proper spelling or capitalization?

Devin SRB: So critical. Can we please meet up to discuss the social at least?

Devin SRB: was that a proper sentence? i'm a sports management major, so I wanna make sure.

I didn't ask.

Devin SRB: Damn, Your Highness. So fiesty.

That was perfect grammar. I'm free Sunday before my meeting.

Devin SRB: what are you doing tomorrow night?

I'm not sure why everyone is so concerned about my Friday night plans, I typically never had any, or anyone asking. Now I felt like a complete bore if I were to tell that to Devin. I'm also not sure why I care what he thinks.

Probably because you have a crush on him, idiot.

He is so quick at texting back I hardly noticed that it is almost 11 p.m. when I look at the time. I have an early class the next morning so I silence my phone. I could've told him that, but I also want to seem a bit mysterious— thinking this is exactly how Frankie would play it off.

I text her quickly— telling her I will think about going out tomorrow night but that I wouldn't know until I knew how much work I had over the weekend. Between school and the sorority it was usually a lot. Especially, since my grades in multiple of my classes were hanging a little lower than was comfortable for my overall grade point average calculation.

The tea I drank starts to make me drowsy, so I try to stifle the large yawn and thrust my mug into the sink to rinse it off under the hot stream of water. Before setting it in the gray drying mat on the counter. I double check the locks on my door, then I shuffle deep into my comforter carefully rolling Hubert around as I do— he argues with me through a few grumbled meows. I set the alarm and place my phone on the charging dock on the nightstand. Sleep finds me quickly, like it always does on days when I often run on a few hours of shut eye and a bucket of caffeine.

Chapter Eight

Friday

DEVIN

I roll over to check the time again on my small alarm clock.

3:30 a.m.

Only 45 mins this time. The longest duration my eyes remain closed most nights is three hours. Even then, that was weeks ago.

In an effort to distract myself from the fact that Elle hadn't ever responded to my last text last night, I stayed up to play Call of Duty. Not exactly the answer to help my insomnia, but it had helped the hours pass.

Eventually, I told myself she had fallen asleep and that I should do the same. That was at midnight. Then images of fists flying and Elle's brown bob fanning around her as she spun at the end of my fingers mixed in a terrible sequence in my mind. So sleep was a fighting battle of trying to get images of limp hands resting on the harsh tile flooring extracted from the blue irises that sparkled brightly under a disco ball.

I throw my legs over the side of the bed, meeting the cold vinyl flooring with my bare feet. Quickly I grab for my gray sweatpants and black hoodie. Slipping on my gray running sneakers and swiping my white corded headphones off my desk, before heading for the door.

The dark morning air is nail-bitingly cold, and the shiver that runs through my entire spine would have woken me fully if I wasn't already wide eyed. I force my legs to move and jog along the road leading back to the main campus.

Two and a half hours after jogging around the silent academic buildings and slumbering dorms, the slow stream of students starts to flow out. I dodge the few early morning class takers. With just over four hours until my first class, I am itching to take out my phone.

The blank screen mocks me.

I pull up the messages with Elle, that I had labeled "Her Royal Highness". Slightly second guessing my decision to do so before sending off a quick "Good morning" text. Then flicking over to the chains and scrolling down to Holden's name.

hey man, looking for elle. do you know her class schedule?

Holden: Devin, I can't give out students' class schedules.

she told me to meet her, but didn't say where. its for planning the social.

Holden: Check the south admin building.

ur a lifesaver

Holden: If she asks, I didn't send you.

Holden is a good guy, even one I could see myself befriending in a different circumstance. He is only a few years older, but he is also a campus employee. He is more of a confidant than any professor would be; super admirable. One of the few faculty that knows my true history at U of C. I don't remember what exactly he is studying, but he is getting his masters at Conifer Valley while working, so I knew he'd be awake.

The first classes usually started at seven, so I wouldn't be able to make it before it started but I could definitely meet her after. I shower quickly and fly out my door again, unsure where I left my jacket, so I'm embracing the cool morning air as the sun melts away the frost that has dusted a top the grass.

She'd said we could meet on Sunday, but that was too far off for my liking. I want to talk to her today, and the fact that I am not sure what she was doing tonight is causing my mind to stir uncomfortably.

The scent of coffee soaks into my nostrils as I pass the tiny cart that is parked outside the School of Mathematics and Science. This building is a huge reminder of the few classes at my previous university, U of C. Nothing about Colorado really reminded me of the University of Cali, but I miss the classes I had taken there— specifically the major I had selected. I had hid it well from my dad for the first year, until getting kicked off my soccer scholarship had allotted him unwanted inspection of my college activities. To him, mathematics was a useless major— *"Finance would at least have some true life application, Devin."* he'd say often. Him being a self made owner of a construction company made him practical. Even when that business had grown into a full blown home building operation within the first ten years, and had lined my fathers pockets. But it hadn't changed his ideals of being a hard working blue collar man.

It had also made him the size of a house as well, and given him all the right amount of muscle to knock me around when I was not lining up to his ideal life. My mothers passing hadn't helped him become less hostile, but the punches came less often when I showed the potential to become like him.

He stopped hitting me all together one day out of the blue. I wasn't sure if it was because I matched his height or if it was because I no longer did things to upset him. I had eventually done something though, but the last beating sent me to the emergency room. Where I lied between my teeth— saying I had fallen off a ladder while helping my dad paint a house. He had even gone as far as to whip a few streaks of burgundy stain he had in the garage across both our arms and hands to send the story to the presses firmly.

I wanted to believe that my dad wasn't a bad guy, just that he didn't know how to reign in his anger at the worst possible times. Everyday was a constant battle to accept that fact and go back to seeing him, or to keep avoiding his calls.

"What can I get you?" asks the bubbly barista, she looks warm in her large brown overcoat, adorned with a faux fur lined hood.

Unsure what to order for Elle, I ask for my coffee black first. Then request a sugary latte, hoping it is something girls drank.

Coffees in hand, I weave through the glass doors and down the hall of the South Administration Building. Glad to be out of the windy breeze of the morning, as the hot cups warm my palms.

I scour the entire first floor, trying to discreetly look into the small rectangle glass boxes of each door. I'm not sure which class Elle was in, but this building only has three floors and I will check each class room thrice, if I have to, before the period lets out. I keep telling myself it is because I am impatient and stressed about my position. Any other twenty one year old man would be out trying to score with as many girls as they could. I— on the other hand— found the idea of a flightful love less appealing. With each passing breath I was beginning to feel like Holden Caufield, except I was more than halfway attached to Elle. The sight of her spinning on the dance floor. Unraveling the tight stings that held her upright, slowly coming undone under my gaze, is all I can think about.

With great consideration of the coffees in my hand, I quickly vault the stairs to the second floor. I only have a few moments left before students start flooding the hallway and I will be forced to wander, searching for her through the swarm. The second window I peek into reveals to be fruitful, because I see the sight of her in the highest row. Perfectly framed in the crosshatched glass. Laptop firmly in front of her as she types away furiously. I watch her, inamored by the sight of her tucking a stray strand of her brown hair behind her ear. Never looking up from her screen.

The sight of a girl sitting closer to the door catches my gaze, her scowl of disapproval of my snooping evident across her pinched face. I back away, by heart threatening to jump out of my chest. I was too worried about finding her, because I hadn't thought of what I was going to say once I saw her. Also the fact that I have been stalking her slightly— since we haven't spoken much and now I am standing outside the first class she had on a Friday morning, looking all disheveled— was crossing my mind. I find a spot on the far wall, leaning against it and allowing for the perfect view of the class— for when it empties— because I want to ensure I won't miss her.

My phone begins to buzz alive in my pocket and I am grateful my hands were already preoccupied with the two mugs of hot beverages. The vibration continues on, then pause before incessantly continuing again. Now, I definitely know who it is.

Students began to fill the hall, indicating the end of the class period. I shift on my feet to ease the anxiety out of my shoulders. Concerns about many different things start to shape in my head. Had I brushed my teeth? Would she like the cologne I wore? What if she hated coffee all together?

Time freezes. The world becomes a haze of bustling bodies that shuffles around the crowded hall, and my mouth falls open at the sight in front of me.

Elle's delicate features appear through the gaps in the students as they file out of the classroom. She is so pretty, her soft brown hair framing her face. Nothing about her is below average, her entire presence sending tingles through my arms. I watch, dumb struck as she hikes her tote bag higher on her shoulder.

Oh I'm a goner, far worse than H. C. had ever been. Salinger was right about falling for an angel like her, I was going crazy.

She was making me crazy.

Big blue eyes lock me in their grasp, and the coffees threaten to leave my hands. I force myself to remain firm, unmoving as I watch her glide towards me. For the second time in my life, her entire focus is on me. An inevitable grin spreads across my face. If only a soft country song was playing now— so that when I told this story to our future children— it would have set the mood better. Instead the sound of voices filling the air muffles the first words out of her mouth, I stare blankly. My mind is empty, this girl could reduce me to miming.

"Say something idiot," my mind screams.

Chapter Nine

Friday

ELLE

Devin SRB: Good Morning.

I fly around the kitchen— making my tea, then cleaning up any remnants of my residence in my own apartment. I like when things are in the correct place, my therapist says it's my way of controlling aspects of my life after my parents divorce. My mom is also extremely tidy, so I also blame the obsessive nature on her caretaking.

My mom is my best friend. I love everything about her— except that she stayed with my dad for too long. She told me this when I turned eighteen. That she stayed too long— for me. I was sure that the fighting between the two of them had just become too much, but in fact she had been miserable for years. I don't think she told me in a way to make me feel responsible, but a small part of me felt a bit guilty.

She is living her best life, being single now after many years in a loveless marriage and I admire her for that. I want her to be happy. I want her to be able to live in her own house and buy all the food she wants, because a small part of me felt like she was finally letting herself do that. Which is why I acted like I was completely fine with the fact that she was going to Mexico with her friends over the Thanksgiving break. I told her I couldn't come home anyways, that I had too much school and sorority work, but truly, I was a bit disappointed.

I loved all the holidays surrounding my family and food, especially back home when we still lived close to every other person that made up our close family circle. Our small farm style home, a few blocks away from my grandparents and only a short drive further to my aunt and uncles.

My mom had sold the farm this past summer— as soon as her divorce was final— and fled her old life in pursuit of refinding her happiness. Used the money to buy herself a nice townhouse in Edina. A quaint suburb of Minneapolis, that had a *"cute little indoor rink"*, she had said. Describing how she drove past it everyday on her way from her gym and the brewery she met her friends at for happy hour. She had also said it to make me more optimistic about the move, but all it reminded me of was that my room used to be something I thought I'd come back to one day and admire. Like a cheesy romcom I had watched growing up, one where the parents stayed together and lived in their honeymoon home that they had purchased on a whim. With a realtor telling them "this one is perfect for a growing family", and "the neighborhood will be great. Just right for growing old in". Not, "oh yeah, it'll be worth a pretty penny when you divorce in twenty five years". "A real profit", she'd say with a wink, because in my head everything mild in humor had to be driven home with a wink or a tilt of the head.

I brought what I needed to Colorado— Hubert included— everything else we donated or sold. Including my glorious white and tan barbarian pinto horse, Rosie. She was the hardest thing for me to leave. Second to my mom. I understood that a horse— with such a few years behind her mane— needed to go to a loving family with children that would ride her everyday. Pets are an interesting concept. Only people that have cherished that companionship truly understand even though they are a short lived chapter for us, that our pets live with the soul they love most for their entire lifetime. Our hands hold the power of love or neglect. Rosie is stamped into my skin, literally, I had gotten a tattoo of a rose across my ribs the day I turned nineteen to commemorate our time together forever. It was the first of many tattoos I got, the feeling was an addicting one.

The money from moms sale and the few hundred dollars from her a month kept me going, but I'm not sure what to do next semester— when I will be living off of Ramen noodles.

I slid on my black combat boots— tucking my dark blue skinny jeans in— then loaded my tote bag full of all my folders. Double checking that I didn't leave any behind, before flying out the door sending Hubert a farewell a I go— he's unfazed, sleeping in a giant lump on my gray couch.

I make it to campus in record time but after having to circle around waiting for someone to leave, I am a few minutes late to my Leadership Issues class.

Nate's brown eyes find me instantly as I sweep through the doors. He's wearing the same sweatshirt from a few nights ago. Since hockey seems to be our common interest, I should probably look up his team's statistics or something. I find the last seat in the back, high up on the rows that are constructed with the audience facing the white board. Professor Ford is still shuffling around with the cords to her laptop, indicating I have a few seconds to spare.

Nate appears in front of my row of tables, his height matching up with my gaze as I sit.

"Hey Elle," he smiles and I have a hard time not noticing a few odd looks. The girls in the row in front of mine glance back at our interaction. "Thanks for the notes."

"Hope they helped," I say, pulling my laptop out and my heart sinks at the large number of emails I received so far.

"Pop quiz today," Professor Ford begins writing on the board with a squeaky marker, in an attempt to quiet the murmurings from the rest of the students, "everyone settle in."

"Guess we'll see," Nate reaffirms his statement with a wink while running his hand through his dark hair, before he turns to sit with his friends. I recognize a few of them as my other neighbors— and his roommates— but Nate is the only one I have ever spoken to.

I know about sixty percent of the answers on the test so I hold a dreadful feeling in my gut for the remainder of the class period. Which only grows worse after I get a text from my mom reminding me why my money issues are becoming stressful.

Mom: How's the job hunt going honey?

Fine. Nothing available yet.

I hate lying to my mom but it was easier than explaining that no off campus job was willing to work around class schedules and all the sorority meetings. She will inevitably tell me I am working too hard and that maybe I could give up some of the responsibilities at the sorority, but I don't want that. I like how successful I am at running my chapter, there is a constant level of respect that comes from the other board members. And even though most of the chapter never invites me to anything, I am content with that because the sorority is thriving and I play a hand in that.

The rest of the period is uneventful, but as I take a step into the hall— following the crowd of students all sporting smiles and murmuring about the quiz results— the sight of the man leaning against the wall makes my heart leap.

Devin, all six feet something of him, is leaning his back against the gray brick wall. His dark tee shirt is a different variation of the band tee he had worn the other day.

"Coffee?" His voice jumps from him as he pushes off the wall, before closing the distance between us.

"Sure," I stammer, looking around him for someone to jump out and yell *"surprise"*. I'm not sure exactly why, but after our text conversation last night, I wasn't expecting him to be here. Waiting with two white coffee cups in his hands. Resting with such a casual matter outside my first class of the day.

"I wasn't sure how you drank it, so I got it–."

"Black, is fine." I interrupt, mostly to ease my stress but also because this act is something out of those cheesy rom coms I had watched in high school. And I'm not sure if he realizes that.

He quickly glances at the scribbled letters on the side of the cups, then hands me one, and the smile he shares with me at his satisfaction is heartbreaking.

"Stop doing that." I say, shifting the hot paper mug between my hands.

"Doing what?" he laughs, and the smile decorated with his small dimple never falters.

"Smiling like that."

His hazel irises trace my face, and a blush creeps up to my cheeks. I swiftly turn on my heels and head towards the staircase. He chuckles a response then jogs the few steps I have put between us with ease.

"I texted you," he says, as we emerge from the building. The swarm of students leading like ants out and around campus.

I pull my phone out of the side pocket of my tote. Notifications of all types are displayed and I scroll through them quickly.

"I didn't see it." I lie, exhaling a breath as I stop to face him now. The fresh air makes it easier for me to get my bearings. I need to be professional. So what if we had shared a dance or two at Silver Spur a few nights ago, and that he had texted me last night. He was the SRB Social Chair and he was focused on getting the social event planned. I had to admire his dedication a little. I was a terrible social chair, because it had been hell trying to get a hold of all the fraternity men. The complete 360 degree turn of the scenario is a bit confusing, but also refreshing.

"I said we could meet on Sunday-" I lose all intelligence when I look up to find him looking down at the phone in my hand. His striking features flex as if he's biting his tongue. We are almost touching— almost as close as we had been on the dance floor, all that is missing is his searing fingers on my waist. I back away swiftly, attempting to hide my obvious embarrassment.

"I know," he brushes the few damp blond bangs back off of his face, his biceps flexing and gripping my attention. Why is he so unbelievably attractive? And why is he always slightly wet? I glance away quickly, hoping my face isn't completely transparent.

"Is everything okay?" I shove out, forcing my voice to remain calm, but it comes out breathy.

His eyes fall to my lips before jumping back to meet my gaze, I glance around us again— to avoid holding their contact. Students flutter around us, completely unaware of the tension.

"I told you, I wanted to see you again," he says.

"I thought you were joking." I retort, before a shudder runs through me. My thin KSI embroidered crew neck is doing little to fight off the morning breeze. I know by lunch I'll be removing it, but standing on the sidewalk in front of Devin as he gazes down at me I am frozen. I take a large gulp of the coffee he had brought me, remembering I hadn't shared my gratitude yet.

"Thanks for this, too."

"Of course." He says firmly, his dimple appearing briefly with his smile, before I turn to begin walking.

As he starts off alongside me, I try to remind myself that we are professionals here, that I need to focus on the Greek business. Not that he had gotten me coffee— he most likely bought lots of girls coffee. The faster we planned this social event, the faster he could stop worrying about bringing me coffee, and he could go back to doing whatever it was that frat guys did.

"Um–" I start to say, to avoid our silence.

"Do you have another class?" he interrupts.

"No." I say, turning to him slightly. He didn't seem to notice the chill in the air, his firm hand gripping his coffee sans cardboard koozie. My eyes catch on the writing. Noting it is some sort of latte with a very long listed name of flavors. White chocolate, macadamia, maybe?

"Where are you going then?" I force my eyes to the path in front of us, noting how he glances at me everytime he speaks.

I realized then, for the first time in weeks, I don't have an intended destination. Devin is like a meteorite, flying into my life at random times and disrupting my focus.

"Uh..the library." I say, forcing myself to make a decision. Even though I hardly ever went to the library to work. The tables were always overflowing with groups of students, but the student life office would be filled with Greek Life members at this hour. So the library would have to do it for now. At least until my meeting at noon.

"Perfect," he exclaims, "me too."

He doesn't carry any sort of bag or books. He walks through campus, my polar opposite. Carefree, and blowing where the wind takes him.

"Why?" I ask, realizing my tone is harsher than intended.

"We have a meeting." He's tilting his head and smiling again.

"Stop doing that." I huff, uncomfortable by his constant grin. I'm not sure what the hell is going on, but I also note how odd I must look walking next to this extremely hot individual who smiles like the Cheshire Cat constantly.

The laugh that escapes him is loud, and the boisterousness of it catches the attention of students walking in the opposite direction. "Doing what? Exactly, Your Highness?"

He jogs ahead, not seeming to care what my response is. He grips the handle of the glass doors before flinging it open and holding it for a few people as they exit. Before waiting for me to walk through the threshold, he leans his head against his knuckles where they hold the frame.

The echoing of voices in the hall leading to the Conifer Valley auditorium in front of us are loud, so we weave through students silently. He catches my elbow and drags me out of the way of an oncoming group of large men. I pump into his side, but he doesn't let go, instead he pulls me across the front of him and tucks me under his other arm. The act is swift, like his dance moves. The intimacy of the act surprises me, and I shove out from under his grip.

Placing a heavy distance between us once the area in front of us is cleared, I can see the internal entrance to the library in front of us— the sign on the door indicating no open drinks other than water were permitted. I throw back my head, swallowing a few gulps of the lukewarm coffee before tossing the rest in the garbage can at the door. Devin tosses his cup in after mine, then grips the door handle and opens it.

The library is full to the brim— every table is fully occupied by groups of students in various sized study groups. The main floor in front of us even has a large group all oriented towards portable white board. A dark haired girl in a dark maroon sweater and black mini skirt points out the equations on the board. The letters look like a foreign language— one I'd never be able to understand.

I catch Devin's gaze fixated on the girl, and a slight pang of jealousy rips through me before I force myself to pick up my pace. Of course he is easily distracted by girls in mini skirts. I wipe my sweaty palm in my dark skinny jeans before forcing myself to walk over to the stairs. My steps are the only sound in the space, until I hear Devin jumping up them a few at a time to catch back up with my pace. I force myself not to care where he had been for the last few minutes— forcing my eyes forward as I find an open table in front of the large windows facing the Rocky Mountains.

The sight of orange and yellow trees dancing at the base of them, reminding me that autumn in Colorado is unlike anywhere else. I force my tote bag into one of the chairs then sit in another, pulling out my laptop and opening it. Devin fills the chair across from me, pulling out a paperback copy of 1984 by George Orwell that I hadn't seen him carrying and his phone. He places both on the table, phone face down on top of the white book cover, before sliding it away from him and leaning forward on his elbows. His hazel eyes flutter over my laptop and I realize he is trying to read the stickers I have used to decorate the lid.

He looks up over the screen and begins to smile.

"Stop smiling at me like that." I whisper.

This only makes his smile widen as he leans closer—his chin hovering over my blank laptop screen. "Got something against smiling, Your Highness?"

"No." I shift my eyes down, and force myself to open my email. Then to another widow with a word document. I hadn't had time to create the folder I was going to keep for the social chair yet, so I don't have anything else for this impromptu meeting.

"Okay, what have you and Lacy already discussed for the social?" I start and he leans back in his chair. His biceps flex again as he laces his fingers and clutches them to the back of his head. He glances out the window at the view briefly. "Nothing."

"Great," I huff, "so starting from scratch then?"

We go back and forth like this for about a half an hour—me asking questions and him giving me one word answers. I attempt to look solely at my computer screen and not at his penetrating gaze. The few times that our eyes do meet,

I quickly shift mine away, but can still feel his burning my skin.

We settle on a bowling social, it'll be easy to set up last minute with the local alley— which Devin offers to do— and we agree there is no need for decorations. We will each chip in part of our budgets to purchase a few appetizers for each lane. No alcohol permitted because it's too much paperwork. Then after the first round is done, if people want to stay for another, they can pay for it themselves.

I flip through all the windows on my screen, glancing again at my calendar and noting the meeting I have in an hour, and dreading the name that sits in the title.

Trent.

Who liked to have one on one meetings every once and a while and over lunch— specifically on the second Friday of the month. At least this time I would be able to have something other than his proposal to discuss while he watches me chop down the small salad. I hated eating in front of his judgmental stare.

Hoping he will message me to cancel, I check my phone. I scroll through the texts to find his name, before sending off a message to confirm we were still good to meet. He responds immediately saying he'll be there early but has to make it short today. Meaning I would also need to be there early— more specifically— in less than a half hour.

"Boyfriend?" Devins voice is no longer a whisper.

"I don't have a boyfriend." I say, before shoving my phone back into the pocket of my tote bag. Devins smile indicates where I had made the mistake, and I immediately try to hide the embarrassment caused now that he has bested me.

"I know." He's all confidence wrapped in an annoying package.

"Then why'd you ask?"

"I wanted to hear you say it." He leans in on his elbow again. His hazel eyes tracing my face, pausing on my lips briefly. "So you'll have dinner with me?"

"No," I say quickly, "and I have to go."

I close my laptop, only after checking if it is sleeping one last time. Before tucking it in my bag.

"I guess, I'll see you next Thursday for the Social, then." I say, "If there's any issues with the bowling alley, you can text me."

"Platonically?" He adds, ignoring my parting words. His phone begins to buzz.

"You can get that." I say, beginning to stand.

He ignores his phone, standing to face me. "Elle?"

"Devin?" Something flashes behind his eyes, before he fixes them on my nose.

"I need to properly apologize for hitting you in the face," he whispers, lifting his hand and grazing the bridge of my nose with the back of his forefinger.

A shudder rips through my spine at the soft contact.

Until I remember who he is. Who I am. I force myself to push away from him. His hand falls to his side. He grabs his phone, typing something quickly and meeting my gaze again.

I feel my phone buzz against my rib cage, pulling it out to see a text from him.

"Great," he whispers, "so it does work."

I stand there, mouth slightly open, gawking at him as he turns away to leave.

Unsure if I am shocked by his entire presence, or the small moments that seem more than platonic.

Frat boys do this, I tell myself.

They flirt and sit through meetings with no other goal than to eventually get you to have dinner with them. They sit there smug and foreboding.

But Devin also opened doors, and pulled me out of the way of being trampled. Cared about the fact that my nose had been slammed into— even if he was the one who had done the slamming.

"Fine," I say, unsure what I'm agreeing to.

"Dinner?" He faces me again, shoving his book into his back pocket.

"As friends." I clarify, folding my arms over my chest.

"Tonight?" He steps closer again.

"Sure," I say, turning to retreat. Completely unsure what else I could say, I start to walk away. Not wanting to reveal that the man I definitely have a crush on just asked me to dinner.

Attempting to remain calm as I turn to face him again, "text me the details."

The smile he sports somehow manages to be larger than the rest I have seen prior to this moment. Two dimples on full display and his hazel eyes are glistening.

I turn again, pressing my fingertips to my mouth, only then realizing I am also wearing a smile that hasn't appeared in a very long time.

Chapter Ten

Friday

DEVIN

S napping a mental image of her smile.

Snapping a mental image of her ass in those jeans.

Snapping as many mental photos as I can of Elle as she retreats down the stairs and out of sight. Now, I am simply standing here like a lovestruck idiot. I slump back into the chair. Focusing my attention on the seat she has just vacated. Reviewing the play by play of the entire encounter in my head.

She has agreed to have dinner with me.

"As friends."

I blow out a small breath before glancing at my phone. Five missed calls from Dad since this morning. I had two choices here— the first being that I could call him back. Apologize incessantly that I was in class. Or that I forgot to charge my phone and had left it in my dorm. All the things that I could think of though fell flat. It didn't matter what I said he would have the same response. So I chose option two— which is to ignore him for now.

A text from Jinny saves me. I immediately click to open the chain.

Jinny: Darcy! SOS!

i told you not to call me that.

Jinny: It's a requirement now. How's college?

you'd love it, L.J. i'm in the library now

Jinny: Heaven. Also Chuck and Blair kissed, not that you care.

don't. what is the S.O.S?

Jinny: Nothing. I was curious if your Miss Elizabeth has caved yet.

Ah. i get the darcy reference now.

she agreed to dinner.

Jinny: Slow. and AWWW you gonna cook?

maybe.

Jinny's Darcy reference had me all twisted. Pride and Prejudice by Jane Austin was Jinny's favorite novel. Now her favorite movie, as well. I had seen the 2005 adaptation with her thousands of times. She insisted it was a requirement for her to become an English literature major.

The book was better than the movie.

Jinny lives and speaks at the speed of light. She is always running, dancing, and laughing. Every room is heavily satiated on her energy alone. Her appearance is not too dissimilar to my mom— her aunt— before she passed of course. Long blonde hair that swirled around her shoulders or is thrown up in a crazy bun. Reading three books at a time. One she most likely was rereading, something heavy like The Bell Jar by Sylvia Plath— something for fun, she'd say. Then something that warmed her soul— something romance heavy and plot thin or repetitive. If she wasn't inside reading, she was hiking, snowboarding, or rafting. Now that I thought about our last rafting excursion, she had brought a small paperback, *"in case she had to wait in a line."*

Her visiting in a few weeks was a blessing, she was enthralled with the idea of coming to Conifer Valley University. She had even rejected some other major named universities to be able to come here. I had told her about Elle— after I had elbowed her in the face. She had reminded me to be a gentleman. The weight of the statement has not registered to her. I was a gentleman and nothing like my father.

I had also told her that we had slow danced at the Silver Spur. She was overjoyed and already asking what our apartment looked like. I didn't have the heart to tell her that Elle was still a very tightly wound yo-yo— one that I haven't untangled yet.

Dinner. I'd need to cook dinner to impress a girl like Elle. She was president of her sorority, something I didn't take lightly in the slightest. She was a beacon that an entire group followed. Like Trent, she demands attention— respect— and I wanted to do that justice. I didn't want her to know that I was going to cook her dinner though.

Mostly because I didn't know what I would even make, or what she liked to eat. I couldn't ask right out, but I also couldn't ask her " where do you want to go tonight." A heavy weight dropped in my stomach. I had absolutely fucked myself, because now I needed to plan a dinner in one night. And to think, I'd actually planned to make it to my lecture today.

I fire off a text to Elle, hoping that she will respond soon. I don't even know if she has a kitchen. I certainly don't.

Her Royal Highness: "asking for a friend. is steak something sorority presidents eat?"

"I'm a vegetarian."

I was too confident about my message, so confident that I even stood up from my chair and started heading back to my dorm room. Until my phone buzzed and the message stopped me from leaving and resulted in my pacing the rows of the library stacks instead.

"Fuck," I mumble. Of course she was a vegetarian. Most likely one of the ones who chose the lifestyle to "save the environment." I could do this— a challenge of sorts. To cook something that wasn't for carnivores like myself. I was out of practice on the basics, I had only cooked with another person too, I wasn't like I did it everyday. Unless making creations in my microwave counted as culinary masterpieces.

do they have vegetarians in italy?

Her Royal Highness: Probably.

do vegetarians eat cheese?"

Her Royal Highness: Yes, but I don't like Camembert.

that's french cheese.

but noted.

Her Royal Highness: I'm in a meeting. We can talk later. I'll send you my address soon. I am assuming you're picking me up.

be ready at 7.

Sweet victory was as delicious as expected. I had forgotten to ask if she had a kitchen but when she had finally sent me the address, it only took a quick search on the internet to find the apartment layouts. Each one had a kitchen, some with many other rooms. Hopefully she doesn't have any roommates— I would buy extra ingredients just in case. Pesto Cavatappi, simple, but impressive enough I thought. Plus the other basics, just in case she has a sweet tooth and I needed to make some sort of dessert.

I manage to refrain from plowing over anyone as I run from the library to the parking garage, searching frantically for my car. Until I realize I left my keys in my room, so start to jog back over to that building.

My phone buzzes alive in my pocket, and in my excitement I don't even think before answering.

"Hello?"

"This is the tenth call today, Devin." My dad's icy tone slows my steps to a walk.

"Yeah." I clear my throat. "Been in class all morning."

"Sure."

"What's up?"

"Jinny wants to come early and stay for the entire break."

"That's fine with me." I realized years ago that the shorter the sentence the less likely my dad was to be set off. Silence mixes with static as I wait for him to continue.

"Great," he says, before ending the call.

I shove into my dorm room, quickly digging through piles of clothes and shifting papers on the desk in search of my keys. At a complete loss to where they might appear, I began turning all the pockets out of my pants. Tossing the garments into the bin as I go. Then I clear the desk, organizing the piles neatly, placing pens back into the mug I kept them in. I remake my bed— searching in all the loose folds of sheets for my keys as I do.

My phone buzzes in my pocket, I slouch off the side of the mattress, atop the now neatly tucked comforter. It's a cryptic message from Trent.

Trent: Need you now more than ever, brother. elaborate?

Trent: With the Ice Queen!

I ignore his comment, the sight of sparkling metal beckoning me from under the dresser. I lean down to snatch the keys before I'm running out the door.

Chapter Eleven

Friday

ELLE

I close the door and crumple to the floor. My tote bag drags on the door as I crouch into the seated position. Some days are longer than others— today was an endless loop of class meeting, class, meeting, another meeting, and now finally *rest*.

I unhook my tote from my shoulder, as Hubert comes bounding around the corner of the island, meowing his call to feast. I crawl over to his white barrel of cat food and unscrew the plastic top, scooping out a heapful of dry food. It sings as each pebble hits the bowl, and his fervor of screams heightens.

My phone pings in my tote, and I scramble back on my knees to dig for it.

Devin SRB: on my way.

I chant no at myself a billion times before throwing myself to stand, grabbing the straps of my bag and rushing into my bedroom. I live about three minutes drive from the main campus— so this message starts setting off alarm bells in my head left and right. Luckily my simple apartment is always clean— by a normal person's standard– so I don't even give it a second glance before I am barrelling into my bedroom.

I need to figure out what the hell to wear, and fast. I thought after the last night of scrambling to find an outfit that I'd have this down. I look down at my clunky combat boots, throwing them into the back of my closet and pulling out some black heels I wear for Sunday meetings. Then I flip through all the dresses that I own— I have maybe three. A black one for formal meetings and initiations, a white one from my own initiation, a long maxi salmon number, then my old prom dress. It's touching the floor and covered in sequels, and it weighs about half of one of my legs. So I slid it along the metal pole— further to the back. The black one it is.

I hurry into the bathroom, begin clearing the counter, then pull the small plastic basket that holds all my makeup.

My reflection reveals nothing of promise as I swipe at my skin to figure out how to fix it. Like the black dress choice, I settle for basic. Just a little more eyeshadow and mascara then I typically chose for my everyday look, before finishing with chapstick.

A knock sounds at the door. Huberts meowing ceases as he flees to the bedroom, and I shuffle to the door quickly—only causing him to pick up his pace.

The air rushes from my lungs at the sight of Devin wearing his usual dark attire, but his jeans have no rips, and the dark green tee shirt he has on is new to me. The lettering on the shirt is a thin line of black cursive, scrolling out a foreign language that I don't understand. In his grip are two brown paper bags, which he lifts in some gesture that I am meant to understand.

"You have a kitchen, right?" he asks, a blonde curl falling over his brow. He smiles, as he looks into my apartment before I can answer.

"I thought we were going out?" I say, stepping back and holding the door wider for him to enter.

"I thought I'd make dinner," he says, placing the bags onto the white counter that makes up the peninsula.

"Make me dinner?" I am reduced to short illiterate sentences.

Which only makes him laugh. All humorous sounds cease when he turns. His eyes trailing over my KSI crewneck and skinny jeans. All the way down to my bare feet that I now shuffle uncomfortably across the laminate.

"Is that what you wear out on a date?" he asks, finding my eyes again.

"No," I gruff, before running back into my room and swooping the black dress off my bed. Throwing myself back into the main room dramatically, I say, "I was going to wear this. Also this isn't a date."

"Where are your pots?" his voice trails out from behind the counter, as he leans over to search through my cabinets.

"Above the fridge." I say. I can feel my brows scrunch.

"Why?" he laughs, reaching gracefully to the cabinets hanging high over my white fridge. A sliver of his skin appears under the hem of his shirt as he stretches. Heat rushes up the back of my neck and I stare, mesmerized by him.

I glance away quickly, folding the dress over my arm. "Why, what?"

"Why do you keep them up there?" he asks, as he begins filling the pot he found with water from the tap. "Also yes it is."

"It is what?" I ask, unsure how he feels so casual everywhere that he appears. His confidence is unwavering, and now he is cooking me dinner. While I stand here gaping at him.

"A date." His words are so poised and assertive. Each one followed by a smooth movement of his body. He finishes filling the pot, spins to light the electric stove top with a flick. Then starts looking through drawers and cabinets again. I'm beginning to realize Devin lives like he dances. Smooth, swift, and thoroughly enjoying himself. He probably kisses that way too, I have heard that dance skills directly coordinate to the bedroom.

"Don't worry, I'll find everything. You change into something comfy."

"Comfy," I echo back, hoping I don't appear crimson.

"Yes, now go, Your Highness, I've got it." He says the words like a hidden promise.

Every rom com scene, from every movie I'd ever seen, is playing in my head. I met this man a matter of days ago and already he is in my kitchen, cooking the only true meal that has ever been cooked— other than ramen— in my small apartment kitchen.

Next he's grabbing a small black portable speaker out of one of the paper bags that still sits filled on the counter. He starts a soft pop station from his phone, which trickles through the space and he begins to actually *dance*. He finds my blue cutting board and removes a knife from the block— the one I had only purchased because it seemed fitting in the otherwise spotless kitchen. The sound of him chopping pulls me back to reality.

"I'm more worried about the mess."

"I'll get that too." His handsome smile grips his face again, and the dimple in his cheek appears. "Go," he points towards the door with the knife tip.

I shut the door behind me and scramble to find my phone. I have little to no experience with this situation and I am in need of some serious advice.

What do you do if a man makes you dinner?

Frankie: Fuck him.

Frankie: Wait! Who's making you dinner?

No, it was hypothetical.

Frankie: Ha I almost believe you. Here's a thought...

Frankie: Eat the man's dinner, then decide if you fuck him.

Thanks for the help.

Frankie: I want details tomorrow!

I throw my phone at my pillow. Before rummaging through my dresser drawers to find a comfortable pair of black leggings.

I will not be fucking Devin tonight, I tell myself— but I check my thong color just in case.

After beginning the battle of pulling on leggings, that idea sticks harder than I want it to, making me realize I haven't shaved in days.

So now, I am pressing my bare toes to the white porcelain as cold water flows from the tap— splashing around my feet— as I scramble to shave my stubby hairs as quickly as possible. A hiss escapes me as I nick the small bone on my outer left ankle.

A streak of crimson runs down into the puddle forming at my toes. Panic over what he must have been thinking is taking me so long starts to make me more anxious. I quickly jump from the tub, drying around my legs before attempting, and failing, to pull the leggings on. After a few painfully long moments I am able to get them on. After I sling my arms through a thin black bra to match my thong of course, but also because the thin lacey structure is more comfortable. I find an old hockey T-shirt— from my high school team— and the sight of the cartoon grizzly bear on ice skates printed on the gray cotton is a nice reminder of home.

I adjust my hair in the mirror, up into a small bun, only to shift it back to the down position. I spray myself with vanilla perfume and decide I need to leave the confines of my room— before Devin decides to conquer it as well.

The scent of starch and fresh basil assault me as I walk back into the main space. Devin's left side is to me, and I take it as an opportunity to watch him while he stirs a wooden spoon in the pot on the counter. Every second feels like a stolen glance, one I know will end once he turns. So I step slowly towards the counter and sit atop one of the white soft topped bar stools. He sings along to the song playing through his speaker— confidently missing a word every line or two. But he never stops. Until the song ends and he turns.

I'm not as shocked by the smile this time. It is becoming part of his "look". Dark jeans, t-shirts, and a smile the shape of a crescent moon— bright as the north star. Even his dimple making an appearance isn't as unfamiliar either. I still stare at him all the same— astonished that he is here. He has removed his shoes, and placed them in the small rack by the door. The groceries have been sorted through and most of the bags were folded and tucked behind the bin of trash near the fridge.

"Who taught you how to cook?" I ask, trying to distract myself more than him. But something dark flashes behind his eyes, before he turns to busy himself with the pot atop the stove again.

"My mom."

"Is she a good cook?"

"She was," he says while shoving his hands into my tiny pink oven mitts and gripping the edge of the pot. He twirls and empties the water into the sink— letting the pasta catch in a strainer. Before flipping the spilled noodles back into the pot. "She died when I was eight."

"Oh," is all I manage to say. Unsure if an apology is the right approach. It doesn't feel *right*, so I ask the only thing I can think of. "Did she have your smile?"

"No," he laughs again. This sound is more ingenuine, than every other encounter. I can now differentiate his true one from the one he simply uses to pause time briefly before answering. "Her's is.... was warm and inviting."

"So it is then."

This time his laugh is more of a huff, and he turns his back to me once more. He mixes something into the pot before gripping one of my small blue bowls. I don't have a table, but he doesn't miss a beat— placing the bowl in front of me and delicately laying a fork next to it. He fills his bowl, as I stare at mine. Shocked at the smell of basil and parmesan wafting into my nostrils. He circles around the counter and sits on top of the stool next to me— facing me as he holds the bowl up and smells his artwork.

I find his gaze. Something in my rib cage leaps and I fear it is my heart. I stab the fork into a wiggly spiral noodle, before lifting to blow a cooling breath over them. I feel his eyes on me as I repeat the motion and then dive into the first bite.

"Thank you." The words fall from my mouth and I shovel more noodles in, moaning at the taste of them on my tongue.

I feel his knees hit the side of my thigh, sending a shiver across my spine. Only to be reverberated deeper by his laugh.

"Do that again." His voice is thick.

I turn to face him, unsure what he is asking of me. He places his bowl onto the counter, before reaching across the space separating us, and tugs on my stool— spinning me gracefully to face him. Our knees intertwine, settling into one another like puzzle pieces. His hazel eyes trace my face, then lower to my lips. I let my eyes close and suck in a breath of air through my nose. I let out another shuddering huff and the sound seems to be the one he wants. He leans forward until our breaths are mixing— tangling in silence. Small freckles across his cheeks become clear to me. The pad of this thumb drags across the edge of my bottom lip. Swiping a small amount of pesto with it, before he brings it to his lips and sucks the pad.

A loud knock sounds from the door, jolting me back, I hit my knees against his stool as I stand. A twinge of pain shoots up my leg, but before I can let it affect me I am rushing to the door and flinging it open— immediately feeling the rush of cold air and blinding light from the hall hitting my face.

"Nate?"

Chapter Twelve

Friday

ELLE

Elle's voice went up about twelve octaves. Firmly planted on my stool, I have the perfect view of the doorway. The frame I thought was large is filled with the form of a man. He's slouching slightly, bracing himself on the metal threshold. Deep brown hair damp and falling over his eyebrows. He's my height which is aggravating but more irritating is his tan chest is bare and glistening. My shoulders stiffen, and I try to remind myself that I can't act jealous, but it's difficult. So instead I clear the pasta

Nate— as she calls him— looks like a model in one of those fancy boxer advertisements. The ones that you can't help but notice when they flash across the screen. Complete with his gleaming abs out on display and his low hanging jeans. The man has confidence, but I am used to his type. Some used to say I was a *Nate*.

He leans against the frame, flexing his biceps in a triangle and the smirk across his lips tells me he has already started drinking. I rap my knuckles on the counter and his attention finds me over Elle's shoulder. He straightens his stance quickly—crinkles the corners of his eyes— then turns back to Elle.

"I didn't realize you had a boyfriend," he says, brushing his palm over his chest while doing little to cover his blatant gawking.

"She doesn't," I announce.

"I don't," she says in the same moment, turning her blue irises to me. "Devin's in Greek Life."

"Oh," Nate says, "I was just coming to see if you're going to Lasso's tonight."

Elle's turns to allow for the heated pathway between us. Her mouth falls open, then snaps shut again. Her eyes search mine, then drift to the dishes on the counter. She doesn't want to go, I am not sure if it is because I am here or if she doesn't like Nate. Nothing about her body language is indicating much, other than that she doesn't enjoy the thought of leaving while her apartment is full of items unattended.

"We were just cleaning up dinner, but maybe we will see you there," I say, standing. I grip the small blue bowls, hooking a thumb over each, before carrying them to the sink.

Nate's thin lipped smile is brief, "Okay. Cool," he says, before he turns and walks out of my sight. Elle closes the door, but remains standing next to it, watching me.

"My neighbor," she states.

"Seems nice." I say, watching as my hands tremor, the forks clicking with the dishes. Taking the small yellow sponge that she keeps neatly on the rim of the sink, I pump soap onto it from the sparkling cylinder near the hot water handle— then scrub aggressively.

"That's hand soap." Her voice cuts across the air, then she is closing the distance. Tugging at the small cabinet doors under the sink. I tilt out of her way and she reaches for the blue plastic bottle of dish soap. When she brings it up and holds it out to me our fingers brush— water from my fingertips drips to the floor. She's so close to me, and her presence makes me freeze. She smells like freshly washed clothes and something so sweet and familiar.

My eyes follow a droplet of water as it curves around our knuckles and plummets to the floor, splashing her toes. She shuffles them away from me, and out of sight.

Within seconds she has a small mop, brushing out the small drips with the dry pad. I turn and continue cleaning the bowl I am holding— for the third time. My fingertips soften, as I sneak a glance in her direction, she places the mop back in the closet by the fridge.

"You can just leave them on the drying mat," she says, meeting my gaze. She's observing me with a stoney expression.

"Okay," I turn off the water. Then place the two bowls upside down on the soft gray mat next to the sink. Making sure to not hit the small white mug that is already resting there.

"Thanks for dinner, " she says, shuffling her feet into the small living area, she lifts a neatly folded white blanket from the armrest of the gray couch then refolds it.

I clear my throat, then circle around the counter to the stools on the other side again, before resting against one. "Did you want to go to Lasso's tonight, Your Highness?"

"Oh," she huffs out a small laugh. "No, I don't." I watch her as she continues to pick up other objects then places them in more *preferred* places.

"Do you want to watch a movie or something then?" I say. Hoping she agrees, so we have an excuse to sit on her small couch together. So I have an excuse to stay, because I really want to but saying that aloud is slightly creepy.

"Why?" She says before turning to face me.

I'm sure what she means, probably me being *creepy*, but more so she seems to be rattled by Nate's appearance. All I want is to get back to the seconds before he had summoned all her attention. I want her full gaze back on me, her lips opening for me. The urge to kiss her is overwhelming, even with the sight of the purple bruising pooling under her eye initially making me hesitate. I wanted to give her a positive experience to overlap the negative one. Our first meeting was tarnished— that bruise a reminder of it. A reminder of what I could do to her, that I can hurt her. I really, really don't want to do that.

"Why, what?" I ask, standing. Within a few strides I am in front of her. She doesn't flinch as my black socks meet the pale blue shag area rug. She's not scared I will hurt her, I remind myself.

Her lashes flutter, her mouth falling open, and I gaze down at her pale pink lips. Her tongue brushes over her bottom lip like it did the night at Silver Spur, the sight making every single one of my muscles twitch.

"Isn't there a frat party or something tonight?" Her voice is soft as her chin tilts up.

"Probably," I say. Trent had asked me to go to the "Le Cougar Den", of course, but I hadn't even thought about it since I arrived at Elle's apartment. "Did you want to go?"

"No," she laughs, but it's hollow. Then she steps away.

The space she leaves in front of me feels sour, like I'd said something upsetting. I can imagine why. The way the other members of Greek life speak about her, paints her as distant. A mirage. A passing ship without room for entry, but I don't see that when I look at her, maybe it is her casual attire, or witty remarks, or the fact that we remain in her controlled space. Everything in the exact place it should be— except for me of course. She still looks at me like I'm the one thing out of place. I want to change that.

So I sit on the couch, spreading my legs a bit too casually, for dramatic effect. The sight of her eyebrows scrunching together is definitely worth the theatrics. I am feeling so confident about my decision until a large ball of fluff leaps onto my lap and scares the crap out of me.

Her cat— Hubert as she explains with a giggle— appears out of thin air, which is more surprising because his size isn't something that is an oversight.

"He's very stealthy for beings so f–" I look up, Elle has her hands on her hips and a brow raised.

"So?" she huffs.

"Um—" this is a test, I have never had a cat before, so I don't know the proper procedure. It does seem however, that much like a dog, this cat wants his belly rubbed, because he rolls on to his back, spreading across my crotch as I stare down at his fluffy form writhing on my lap. "Flirtatious," I suggest.

"He thinks you're going to feed him."

"Do you want me to?"

"No," she laughs again. I realize quickly that that laugh is the one I could chase until my last dying breath.

"He's had enough food."

"Right." I agree, my arms still spread wide, as Hubert rights himself and leaps back to the floor.

With a sigh of relief my shoulders relax.

"You don't like cats?"

"It's not that," I argue, brushing some stray hairs from my black pants, "just never had one."

"So, a movie?" Elle asks, settling down next to me on the couch. She pulls her feet up, causing her torso to shift slightly in my direction. Tucking them underneath her as she lays the blanket across her lap. She's so close, and my heart is palpitating.

"Sure." I say, trying to ease my heart's pace. Her knee brushes against my thigh and I reach for the corner of the blanket to cover my sudden bulge. Shifting my pants to adjust the boner that starts to form, I curse internally at my body for betraying me.

I told myself that kissing her was the goal for tonight, but now I don't think my control is as strong as I thought. Especially if she stares at me again, her eyes telling me yes, yes, yes. I tell myself that she needs to say it, and if she doesn't want me— I have to accept that.

In an attempt to distract myself, I flip through a mental list of typical first date questions. Since this is in fact a date, I had prepared a little. None of the options seem fitting in this situation though— too random. Now I am starting to worry that she is uncomfortable with the silence.

"Where are you from?" I blurt out.

She glances my way, a small curve pulling at her lips, as she clicks the small remote that controls the multiple streaming applications on her television.

"Minnesota, I thought you already knew everything about me?" The soft light casting her shiny dark hair in a faint purple glow.

"I do, just double checking."

"For the test?"

"Exactly. When is that test again?" I smile, and she smiles back. The sight is so real, this is the real her.

"Soon." She says before turning back to the screen and flipping through the options on the screen. "What about you?"

"Oh I don't have a test planned for you."

"Thank goodness," she huffs, "I'm a terrible test taker. I mean where are you from?"

Her demeanor changes, I'm not sure if she's being serious. Like one of those girls who says she is bad at everything, then still wins all the class awards and prom queen. Something about me really hopes she wasn't prom queen though.

"Winter Ridge," I say, hoping she'll be familiar enough with Colorado ski towns.

"Oh, like Trent." Sudden shock rolls through me, I know she knows Trent but to know that much about him.

"Yeah, actually, we went to high school together." I say, scrunching my brows. We hadn't talked about Greek life yet, I was worried she would never mention it. Only making me more curious about what makes her tick. So often she is working away on the sorority business, but now— now she seems to not want to talk about it at all.

"Do you like being President?" I ask, adjusting my body slightly.

"Um, Archon," she laughs shallowly, her wrist hoovering slightly as she holds the remote up. "We call it Chapter Archon in our Sorority.

"Is it like that with all sororities?"

"I'm not sure, I guess. I never picture myself in a sorority so I'm still learning about them as I go."

"I don't know much either." I am unsure if her statement tells me more or even less about her.

"This one?" She nods towards the screen. I glance briefly to notice it's a rom com I have already seen with Jinny.

"Sure." I say, and the movie begins. I don't think she will answer my question, until she turns her gaze to me and she opens up— the words tumbling out like rain drops.

"It's hard to explain," she huffs a small breath, "I am grateful that my chapter elected me. That they saw something in me that resembled someone they respected. I was worried it was a popularity contest, and till this day sometimes I still think that my endorsement from our previous president sealed the deal. But now, I'm not sure–" The movie's title sequence begins, it's poppy music stopping her briefly.

"Some days it's really hard to remember who I was before all of the position stuff. Luckily I met Frankie before, but most of the sisters see me as their '*boss*'". She uses air quotes when she says boss, and I can see the pain flash across her face. "Someone who can punish them, so they don't even invite me to hang out with them." She sits back and a sniff escapes her. She isn't crying, she is simply stating the facts in front of her, seemingly at peace with the situation as it was.

"What about the other night?" I ask. We hadn't talked about the dances at Silver Spur either, but as I spoke I realized that conversation with Elle was like breathing air, consuming water, or watching a sunset. It was natural, slightly predictable, but beautiful and special all the same.

She is quick, joking often and at every chance. Now though, after sitting here conversing like we are now, I notice she is authentic, and naturally pragmatic. She is definitely respectable, because she's relatable— never trying to be anything she isn't. I think I am confident— but that my friends— is confidence in its purest form.

"Frankie invited me to that," a small smile tugs at her lips as she says her friend's name. She continues to tell me all about Frankie— Francesca Croft— and I continue to ask her questions about her life. Intentionally steering clear of sorority discussions, unless she brings it up. Which she does but she also asks me about the brotherhood. I explain that it is a *side thing*— something to impress my dad and to connect with people as a transfer student.

Midway through the movie, right before the argument is to occur between the two love interests, she offers to make popcorn, and I don't even try to stop my staring as she passes. The leggings she chose to wear doing something awful for my male brain. Every curve of her hips and ass begging for me to touch them— to dig my fingers in.

Eventually we get on the topic of discussing sports. Hockey from her perspective, and the difference between offsides— how it differs in soccer— and I am thoroughly invested in everything about her. Even when my soccer background comes up, and the air shifts as she realizes it's heavy, she turns away from discussing the topic of playing at U of C pretty quickly. I tell her about my natural gift in mathematics which she doesn't believe at first but then I explain I don't do much of it anymore. She never stops conversing, even when I explain that my dad is making me take Sports Management for its applicability. By the end of the film you'd think we were exhausted but she doesn't stop, and I hang on every word. I learn things about her, like how she used to love Thanksgiving because the food is her favorite.

I tease her about being a vegetarian and not really having anything to eat for that holiday. She parries successfully, laughing at my assumption that she had never tried turkey before. To which I drill her with questions regarding each type of meat she misses most. Bacon had been one she knew she'd never eat again, but had definitely loved it crispy. "Never to the point of disintegration on your tongue, though." she said confidently, like wriggly bacon was for savages.

Another movie begins, and we drift closer together. I find the nerve to grip her hand in mine and am thankful when she swirls her thumbs over the back of my hand. Then we each experiment with small gestures. My nerve endings burn alive under her touch. I circle my fingers inside her palm, tracing the life lines. Everything about the girl in front of me is becoming more familiar. A complete one eighty from every other time we were together, yet somehow always like two flames being drawn together. She looks towards the clock, and adjusts to sit up, pulling her hand from mine.

"It's late," she says, standing.

Her sudden change in demeanor catches me off guard, I am dumb struck for a few moments. She reaches for the blanket across my lap, and I have to quickly reaffirm it over my crotch. Her eyes widen and then her smile peaks out briefly.

"Elle?" I want to call her out for the sudden change, push against the walls that I can see her forming, but I am confused how to tread further. I don't want to leave, but I will if that's what she truly wants. It is late, but it is also a Friday.

"Devin?" she parrots, and my name on her tongue is my undoing.

"This *was* a date." I say.

"I know." She laughs, until my serious expression makes her brows furrow. She lets her arms fall to her side. Her eyes trailing over my seated form on her couch.

"No, I don't think you understand." I say, sucking in a deep breath, I want to stand but I'm still hard. "I want to date you."

"Why?" she asks.

I am stunned before I soften, literally. "I thought that was clear," I say.

"Explain it to me." Her voice is small and I realize she still isn't sure why anyone would pick her. She's plainly told me that she never gets invited places, that she doesn't feel like her chapter chose her. That no one would choose her.

"I like you," I say.

She laughs, but I grip her hand, looping her fingers with mine. She stares at them, her mouth falling open slightly, before her blue irises flash to me.

"Let me repeat that." I say, my voice thicker, every nerve threatening to escape my bludgeoning chest. I tug her hand until her thighs are between my knees. "I like you, there hasn't been a single thing about you that I don't like. I don't think you could convince me that there's anything, truly. You're so beautiful. I want to know everything about you, Your Highness. I want to date you and you alone. I want you."

I said everything that I, as a man, thought I was supposed to. But she continues to stare at me like I have three heads. She opens her mouth to speak, but I interrupt. "Let me show you."

"How?" She says, shaking her head.

"I can't show you all in one–"

"No, how–" her gaze shifts around the room, "do you like me?"

"I thought I made it clear."

"No, no, no ,no–"

"Yes." I say, pulling her on to my lap. She lets me, and I take that as her acceptance of me. Finally she's letting me into the circle she's created just for her. I swallow the lump in my throat. Needing to move my hands, I grip her chin with my thumb and fore finger.

"You," she says, positioning her opposite hand onto my chest, "like me?"

"Yes, Your Highness. Now please shut up, so I can kiss you." I say, closing the distance between us and finding her lips with mine.

Chapter Thirteen

Friday

ELLE

D evin tastes like popcorn and the largest breath of fresh air I've had in sometime.

His tongue eagerly grazing my bottom lip and I part them— allowing him to fully taste me. A small moan escapes me as he grips my cheeks in his palms. Pulling me to him firmly.

I have been kissed before, small pecs with my first boyfriend. You know the type, eager but inexperienced. Even the half decent makeouts with the random homecoming dates were terrible, because they were with boys who tasted like ashtrays or had wandering hands that were unintentional and all too delicate.

Devin tastes much better than that.

His lips and tongue are eager in a way that lights my spine with warmth, but he is also delicate, taking his time to savor it.

To savor me.

Devin wants *me*.

Every second of it makes gallons of heat creep up my neck and into my face. His assertion tugging an anchor deep in my gut, encouraging me to match every stroke of his tongue or turn of his head. The thrill of letting go of control consumes me, engulfing me like his palms around my face are.

He pulls away briefly. My eyelids flutter open, and the sight of his tongue dragging across his lip— as if to taste me in my absence— rocking my soul.

I shift, wanting to take control and motivated to match his confidence. I grind myself across his hardened crotch as I settle myself fully on his lap. His hands twine into my hair, cupping the base of my skull. Before pulling me to him again. This time our lips are more familiar with one another.

Increasing the aggression of his movements slightly, he bucks his hips causing my back to arch. He grinds his firm crotch against the thin layer of my leggings, and the friction causes my legs to clench.

My hands explore his chest, his shoulders, all to attempt to reaffirm myself into reality. Every ridge in his skin, of his large muscular form, is intoxicating. All of it making me completely aware and utterly unsure how I went from the girl who didn't date, to making out on the first date. Devin's presence reminds me of what it feels like to be alive. Free to do whatever I want, kiss who I want—free to be with him. Even if it was just in my apartment. Even if this is our sanctuary, one where we are choosing one another. Even if it's just for this moment.

My fingers find the blonde curls at the base of his neck, before digging into his scalp. He kisses the corner of my mouth, then my cheek. Trailing them down my neck and pressing them further into the croak above my collar bone. My breaths are heavy and my moans grow uncontrollable under his attention, only making him more eager.

My head falls back, my eyelids following. Nothing exists in my mind's eye, but the sight of Devin and his glorious gaze on me. My hips grind instinctively. Devin is kissing me, wanting me, choosing me. I feel his need building between my thighs— the pressure restraining under his zipper as he hardens further.

"I don't have a condom," I rasp, and my eyelids fly wide open at the realization. How quickly I had assumed this was going to lead to sex— I feel my cheeks blare a darker crimson.

"Oh," he says, frozen with his lips to my neck. "We could–," he pulls away, and I settle into his lap again. He doesn't soften. "We could see if Nate's still in, maybe he has one?"

The laugh that escapes me is authentic and I can't stop it once it starts. Tears fall down my cheek, and I barry my face into my palms. His calloused hands find my wrists, pulling my hands down, and his laughter vibrates us both.

"Or we could go get some." I suggest, and my laughter dims.

"No," he says, tucking his chin, his smile curving into a circle as he focuses to calm his breathing. His fingertips tighten around my wrists, holding firm to the moment lost.

I pull back hesitantly, afraid of what his face will reveal. It was inevitable that somehow I would kill the mood. That the idea of someone as handsome as Devin wanting me would inevitably come to an end.

Then to my relief, his hazel irises tilt to meet mine gaze, still full of admiration. His hands relax and brush over my thighs, pushing up further until his thumb skims over my core. Instant pleasure runs through me, and he circles his thumb before pressing firmly into my clit.

My sudden breach at the sensation causes his eyes to hood briefly before he tilts his head back. The groan that escapes him is all I need to reaffirm that he wants this. He's holding back because of me. He's a gentleman through and through— unsure how to fix things but always apologizes anyways. Now he's attempting to give, even when we are both afraid to fall. Especially after we hardly know one another.

My breath hitches— making him feral once again— and I nod. He flips me onto the couch again before he settles onto his knees, between my legs. With quick fingers, he finds the waistline of my leggings, pulling them down as he grips them with firm fists.

Tugging them until they are inverted and catching on my ankles. He kisses my thighs as his fingers delicately remove each foot from their hold. His gaze turns back to my core, trailing over my thin black thong, then tracing over my tee shirt and up to my face again.

"If I don't taste you soon, I'm going to implode."

"What are you waiting for, Handsome?"

His hands run up the sides of my thighs, his fingers finding the fabric hugging my hips. His golden flecked eyes lock on my core, as I grip the edge of the delicate fabric. Shuffling my torso, and easing my thong down to my knees. I move a pointed foot to his thigh as he falls back onto his haunches. He slowly tugs the thong down further over my shins, delicately lifting my leg planted on the ground, at the ankle before removing the flimsy fabric.

Then he shifts to the other, moving my ankle up to his face, then he's kissing along the skin covering the side of my calf until he reaches the thong with his teeth. His eyes fall closed as he drags the thong up and over the arch of my ankle. He eases the leg over his shoulder, making my hips shift and I fall back onto the couch.

Devin wraps his arm around the underside of my thigh, tugging me until I rest on the edge. He rakes his gaze over me and slowly settles his attention on my pussy laid bare for him. He leans in and the warm breath off his lips tingles over my core.

"So wet." He says.

"Devin?" I say in a shallow breath. His eyes peek up to mine, their hazel irises wild. "Please fuck me with your mouth now."

"Fuck," he groans, thrusting his lips into my core before the word leaves them fully.

My back bends hard at the sensation of his tongue flicking across my clit. Thrusting myself towards his face. I shuffle onto my elbows for a clearer view of his handsome face devouring me. My eyes catch on the sight of his fingertips digging into the skin on my thighs as he grips them tight— consuming all my headspace. His eyes flick to mine again as he sucks.

No man has ever gone down on me, and after this I have a feeling no man will match what Devin can do. His hands fall away, and my heels dig deeper into the croak between his shoulder and neck. My knee falling open for him further. Lips still clamped onto me, he drives a single finger into me, and it's not enough.

"More," I beg.

He retreats, then digs another one in along with the first. All strength in my body gives out and my elbows shift away from me. My back hits the couch and my arms fly over my head to anchor onto something— anything. Warmth grows inside me, my muscles constricting. A heavy moan penetrates the air, as Devin inserts a third finger, thrusting and sucking in tandem.

"You're so hot," he gasps against my skin, and I groan at his pause.

His words completely undo me, instinctively I clamp harder around his fingers. My toes curl as they dig into his shoulder and the couch.

Devin flicks his tongue over my sensitive skin again, his fingers brushing along all the right nerves inside my core for a couple more beats, then I'm tumbling over the edge as my body trembles around him.

"I'm coming," I gasp.

Chapter Fourteen

Saturday

ELLE

"Do vegetarians eat these?" Devin asks, hoisting a bag of potato chips over the isles for me to see. His voice echoes across the small and very empty gas station we had driven to.

After he made me come all over his face, we realized very quickly that we did in fact need to go purchase condoms. Unfortunately that meant for me to drive us to the closest gas station— also one that was open after midnight.

"Yes," I say, shifting my gaze to the rows of colorfully wrapped candy bars. I settle for a couple kinds, then make my way around to the chip isles— where Devin is reading the ingredients labeled on the back of a bright yellow bag.

"We don't need to buy the whole store," I say, glancing at his other arm which was piled full of other brightly colored bags that are mostly bursting with expanded air.

"You said we can't just buy condoms." He announces, looking down at me, the dimples and twinkle in his eyes making me blush. I had settled on redressing in the same leggings and my ankle combat boots. It is cold, so I have also thrown on a blue and gray cross-hatched flannel button up over my tee shirt, but under his gaze I'm bare.

My eyes shoot to the man behind the round counter— he doesn't seem to care, but embarrassment flushes through my veins. My face must identify this reaction, because Devin laughs, as he turns and strides towards the checkout.

He piles the food onto the counter and I set the candy bars, two light green canned teas, and the small box of condoms next to them. Devin pulls out his wallet before I have the chance to offer.

"I'll pay you back." I insist politely.

"No need," he says, grabbing the flimsy plastic handles of the bags that the clerk has shoved all the items into.

"But you paid for dinner too." I say, striding to the door to hold it open for him.

"That's kind of how dates work, Your Highness."

I hurdle one leg onto my bumper before twisting to sit on my hood. He leans against it, brushing my knee with his forearm as he settles back. A few snowflakes dance briefly in the light breeze, but otherwise the chill is dull and constant.

"You're a good driver." He says, spreading one of the bags open and searching inside it.

I'm unsure how to respond, so I don't.

"Scared of compliments?" He smirks, flashing me a glimpse into his hazel eyes.

"I'm just not used to them." I don't know why my voice sounds so unsure, "Never really get them, I guess."

"Yeah," he nods, before his stare holds too long on the windows of the gas station. "My dad doesn't know how to give them."

"My dad's a pathological liar." I say with a harsh breath, and his eyes snap to me.

"You don't talk about him much." He states.

"Nothing to say really," I shrug, and his palm finds the curve of my knee. He brushes back and forth while I continue, "he kinda disappeared after my mom left him."

"Why did she leave him?"

"He was always angry, never hitting me or anything, just-." He flinches at the words, then shifts on his heels, rocking the car slightly. " Yelled all the time though."

"They both did. Mostly at each other but if I messed up, I'd hear about it. They both were unhappy and that trickled down, I think." He flashes a slight smile, but I know it's heavy. "I like to say they simply fell out of love. He fell out of love with us, and my mom realized that she deserved more."

"And, you?" His voice is low, one I recognize as anger. He's trying to reign it in.

"Love is work," I say, "and you have to work to show it, earn it, and be gifted with it."

"Very wise." He turns to me, bracketing himself between my legs, and kisses the tip of my nose. He doesn't hesitate— confident in every move— even the ones with me.

"Take a picture with me?" I say, and he smiles at the idea. He turns and I hold out my camera in front of us. My other arm crosses across the front of his neck in a tight embrace and my chin finds the croak of his neck.

When I pull the screen closer for observation, I note that he has two dimples making an appearance. That is addicting– the fact that I made him smile that genuinely.

"Ready?" he asks, and I release him from my grip. He turns to grip my hips, helping guide my boots to the cement. I take it as an opportunity to bury myself into his chest. He holds me to him as my arms loop around his torso— he's warm even in the chilly air. He smells so good too.

We stand there, embracing for a while, holding onto each other, leaning into each other, choosing each other. I pull away first, not wanting him to freeze, he leans in and brushes his lips across the tip of my nose again and my cheeks heat. Then he drops his arms away, gripping the plastic bag off the hood and rounding the car.

He flings the back door of my SUV open, removing the canned drinks, then places the bags behind the passenger seat. I hop into the driver side, start the car, and roll down the passenger window. He closes the door, then hands me the drinks through the opening. A faint buzz sounds from far off, and I realize it was his phone as he glances down and removes it from his pocket.

"One second," he says, before striding away. Towards the trash can that has overflowed onto the sidewalk. I follow his pacing, watch the tick of his smile that he covers with a hand. Notice his shoulders bounce as he lets out a laugh. Before admiring his tight ass in his dark jeans.

His voice is soft and reassuring, as it carries over the darkened fluorescent lit space. From what I caught about his parents, I know it isn't his dad. He had told me he had a hard time living up to his dads expectations, and rarely takes his calls. So the urge to eavesdrop only heightens when he turns back towards the car again, hiding the smile from me.

I glance away quickly, fiddling with the knobs controlling the music. Adjusting the volume up, then back down again to attempt to hear better. Panic begins to rise in my chest at the sound of another laugh, then he walks further along the sidewalk.

I crack my tea open with a hiss, then chug a mouthful down— hoping to ease my anxiety. Regret soaked questions flood my mind, until he turns and strides back towards the car.

He's tucking his phone back into the front pocket of his black jeans when he flings the door open and bends into the seat. I buckle my seat belt, looking up to meet his dimpled smile.

"Is everything okay?" I ask, forcing my voice to remain neutral.

"Yeah," he says, twisting to buckle his belt. He bends his elbow out of the car and grips the roof from the outside. "That was my cousin, Jinny."

"Your cousin." I ask, shifting gears and checking all my mirrors.

"Yeah, she says hi."

"You told your cousin about me?"

"Well yeah, to be honest," he says, tilting his chin down. "She's the one who suggested I cook for you."

"Oh," is the only syllable that I can manage.

The streets are deserted, and the drive back to my apartment is swift. I wasn't sure what I expected from tonight, nor what he was, but he hoists the bags of snacks (and condoms) back up to my apartment. I fumble with my keys while he waits patiently. Then when we finally get back inside, he heads right for the kitchen to begin unloading the contents onto the counter.

"What else did you tell her about me?" I ask, removing my boots and placing them by the door.

"I mean," he opens a bag of potato chips. The bag crinkles under his firm grip. "I told her about how we met."

I laugh, striding towards him and shoving my hand into the grease coated bag. He chews his chip, watching me as I place one on my tongue then grab for another.

"She's actually the one who told me to rush and apologize." He licks his lower lip.

"Oh, so you weren't planning on apologizing?" I say, throwing a chip into my mouth after the words, to hide my grin.

"No, Your Highness," he says, placing the bag of chips on the counter top. "I was planning to. I just–", he stops. Then shifts his stance, bracketing me in between him and the counter. Coaxing his hips to mine, and pressing my ass into the counters edge. "Was so panicked that I may have hurt you, that my mind went blank."

"And you always listen to what other people tell you."

"Women like you." His hazel eyes scan my face. The heat of his gaze forcing me to crumble, I grip his forearms.

"Like me?" I whisper.

"Yeah, forces of nature like you." He kisses me, softly. Then whispers, "I'd follow you off a cliff if you asked me too, Your Highness."

The words that came out of this confident man terrify me, but they also make me feel more fortified than ever.

"Devin?" His eyes find mine, and the heat from the moment on the couch rekindles. He bites his lower lip, and nods.

"Fuck me."

He nods harder. Then his palms grip my ass— lifting me— and my legs wrap around him. He carries me, trailing kisses down my neck as he steps around Hubert, who is dancing at his feet. I stretch my hand for the box of condoms on the counter. A laugh escapes my lips, as he groans again, before he hurries us into my bedroom. His stubble tickles the palms of my hands as I press kisses to his lips. His cheeks, his nose. Repeating every gesture he has granted me. Darkness envelops us and his hip crashes into my dresser, and the box of condoms hits the floor.

He places my ass directly on the wooden surface and I gasp at the sudden disconnect. He flips the light on and finds the space between my legs, gripping behind my knees to pull my core against his stomach.

He brushes the fabric of my flannel up and over the curve of my shoulder, then down my arms. Lifting the hem of my shirt— never looking away as he discards that too. Throwing them to the floor in a heap of cotton. Delicate fingers brush over my skin— along my bra straps.

I reach for his waist band and unbutton his jeans. Before driving my hand under the fabric of his maroon briefs, palming his hard cock.

His eyes fall at the gesture— watching me stroke him, before his head falls into my shoulder.

He whispers my name— chanting it until he straightens and attempts to pull away.

"Wait," I beg, and his hooded eyes find my face. "I want you to fuck my mouth."

He groans and my mouth is wetting at the thought. His expression only drives more confidence in me. He steps away from the dresser as I jump down, driving my toes into the carpet.

He unzips his jeans at an agonizingly slow pace, then lets them fall off his hips. Before gripping the back of his t-shirt with a firm hand and tugging it up and over his head. Stipping it from his body.

"Do you want to sit or stand?" I say taking my time to trace over his crotch with my eyes, as he grips his cock through his briefs. I don't really care what his answer is, wanting to see him fully. His hazel eyes rake over me again, before stopping at the space between my black lace covered breasts.

"I'll stand," he says gently while gripping my chin, "are you sure?"

I grin and bite my lip. He won't push this unless I tell him— which sends a warm flush through me at the thought. "Devin?"

"Elle?" He parrots.

"I want you to fuck my mouth." I say again, my voice is thick with the command.

He's pushing his briefs down immediately and my mouth falls open at the sight of him. He grabs his huge cock and pumps it a few times. I fold to my knees in front of him.

"Tell me if you need to stop." He says as his thumb grazes over my bottom lip and tugs my chin down. I open my mouth and he slides his calloused digit in and over my flattened tongue. His eyes trace the movement as he gently presses it deeper, inching to the back of my throat.

"Suck," he growls and my lips clamp shout over his knuckle. Then I do just that— I suck. My back arches and my thighs squeeze tight. His confidence is penetrating my soul, encouraging me to meet his every move. My body reacting to every pleasure his face expresses at the sight of me kneeled at his feet.

I think this is the handsomest he has ever looked. I stare at the tiny tattoos scattered across his torso, as his finger glides in and out of my lips. Many of them have images and patterns I don't understand yet, but I desperately want to decipher them. I reach up and trace over the number twenty two he has in bold letters across his left ribs, and his abs are stiff under my attention. I admire the sight of his neck chains dangling, the curve of his pecks, his hardened core and the muscles that trail down towards his crotch, driving home the sight of his large cock firm, and all for me. I don't have a ton of experience, but from what I have seen and researched, he looks very well endowed. I drag my fingers down his muscled skin and then grip his cock in my hand.

He removes his thumb from my mouth and I swiftly replace it with the head of his cock. Brushing the soft skin over my bottom lip, then over my tongue. The warmth of his precum sweetens my taste buds. He knows exactly what he wants, and I am excited to give into our desires.

His eyes follow the movements he makes with his cock and I feel my nipples harden as he takes in the sight of my mouth on him. The palms of my hands find the sides of his thighs and I press my head forward, taking him half way into my mouth, testing my limits, then gliding my tongue along the underside of his cock. Tracing every groove back to the tip, where I swirl over the head— exploring him.

He groans, and I press forward again, taking him all the way to the back of my throat. My eyes water, but the sensation that pulses through me is unexpected and highly welcomed. I'm loving how he feels inside my mouth— love knowing this is making him weaker.

His hands grip the back of my head and my fingers circle around the base of his cock— my hand twisting and stroking as I continue to suck— working him in tandem.

"Elle." He growls and I thrust him to the back of my throat, gagging loudly. This has to be the hottest thing I have ever done with a man.

He pulls from my gasp, and I pant, stunned he is stopping this.

"I want to fuck your pussy." He says reaching for me, but I am already lifting to stand. "These need to go," he commands, finding my bra's clasp. My breasts fall from their hold with a freeing sensation. Devin's eyes darken at the sight of them. Jumping between looking at my nipples and the center as he tears the condom open with his teeth. I realize quickly that he's obsessed with them and with the tattoo I have on my sternum— making the pain of getting it there completely worth it. He turns us by my hips and guides me to sit on the edge of the bed. I shuffle my leggings and thong over my ass before doing so and he helps drag them the rest of the way off.

"Gorgeous," he says, observing me and tugging on his cock again, gliding the latex over it. He is quick and less gentle this time, which I find even sexier. His ruffled blonde hair falls over his brow and his dimples make their appearance.

He scans my body again, slower, and lazily strokes his fingers over my thighs. Then his hands grip the underside of my knees, flinging them apart before he tugs and my back falls to the mattress. He presses his fingers into the skin on my inner thighs, slowly stretching my legs open for him. He is testing how far I'll stretch for him, so I let my legs fall to the sheets.

His hand falls to my core and with a single thumb he slowly glides over my clit, "You're so wet," he whispers with a rushed breath before his eyes find mine again.

"I know", I respond, unsure if that is the proper retort. His teeth suck on his bottom lip and he guides his hips forward, stroking the head of his cock over me. I shudder when he brushes my clit with the firm head, and my arms give out. The sheets morphing around me, wrapping me further into this ecstasy. My eyes close and my mind clears of all previous thoughts.

"Watch." His voice is thick, and I jump at the command, my eyelids flying open, my chin tucking to do just that as he glides into me.

Slowly at first, but as he realizes he slides in perfectly he drives in harder and I gasp at the sensation. I'm not a virgin by any means but the feeling of Devin inside me, stretching me — seeing him watching me as I take him in to me— is another level of sexy I haven't ever experienced.

He lifts his knee to climb up and drive deeper and I match his movements— shuffling a little further back to allow him to envelope me fully. His elbows meet the mattress next to my head and his weight falls into me, knocking the little breath I had left out of me with a moan. Then one of his hands brushes through my hair sweeping it behind my ear as the other palms my breast. He kisses my chest, my neck, my chin as I let out another sequence of moans and gasps.

He palms me harder, massaging, then pinching my nipple. My hips buck at the sensation and he drives his cock into me further.

"Fuck." I gasp in a breath and he catches my words with his mouth as he bruises me with his lips. The feeling of his tongue brushing against mine making me wild.

My entire body feels like it's going to explode, and every thrust only heightens the burn I feel deep in my gut, each stroke massaging the inside of my soul, pushing me to my release.

He pulls his face away and more words fall out of my mouth, "Fuck. Devin."

"Yes, Your Highness?"

"I'm so close." I breathe, unsure how I will ever reach the climax of this entanglement, or if I want it to end. He lifts back onto his haunches and I'm upset by the lack of contact until he is teasing my clit with his fingers.

"Come on my dick." He says, and I do as he commands— squeezing around him as I combust for him.

Chapter Fifteen

Saturday

DEVIN

"You're gorgeous, you know that?" I ask, my lips kissing every indent of her collar bone. Before trailing them lower until firmly between her cleavage and the tiny tattoo I noticed last night comes into view.

The tiny simple font expressing the truest statement I have ever whispered. *Made in Heaven* is delicately tattooed over the top of her sternum, neatly tucked out of sight unless you are as lucky as a man as I am at this moment. So close my breath causes her skin to flush with tiny bumps, while I kiss the ink softly. Then trail them down, in a scattered pattern under the skin along her lower breast until I reach the delicate rose across her left ribcage.

Her light blue sheets are folded around us, guarding us from the cool early morning air and the rest of our responsibilities. Elle unfolded for me completely, then folded in ways I only dreamed women could do underneath me. Every inch of her is exactly as I hoped she would be, but more so tenfold. Every filthy word out of her mouth was exasperated, with a gasp or a moan. Each one breaking a part of my shell off, along with hers. She's addicting, and I can't stop the itch in my fingers— the itch to touch her— even if I begged my maker. None of that matters though, because she welcomed each graze of my finger tips, arching into my touch as if her skin begged me to feel its warmth.

"I am not," she says, her voice the only sound filling the otherwise silent small room.

"Is this our first fight?" I whisper, enjoying the goosebumps that spread across her bare chest and across the delicate skin of her breasts.

Her body tenses and I grip harder to her hips, hoping to reaffirm her in place. The action only makes her shuffle away and out from under me. The hands she had curled into my hair, falling away, leaving phantom tingles in their wake.

"I was joking," the words are heavy on my tongue.

"I know," she laughs, swinging her legs over the side of the bed, her delicate spine shifting as she throws her tee shirt back over her head. Before letting the hem fall to cover her silhouette. The glow of the lamp on the nightstand doing little to help reveal what the hell just happened.

"I'm just gonna go pick up the living area."

"It's 2 am," I huff out after a laugh, falling onto my back.

The glance she throws over her shoulder, before she tucks her soft brown locks behind her ear and stands, is anything but humorous.

"I can help after we get some rest." I press up on my elbows, her soft cotton sheets are warm and I don't really want to get up to chase her. Everything I typically wouldn't do is happening, so I would definitely do just that if she left.

"I feel restless," she huffs, turning to face me in her descent from the room. Her arms lightly fall with a small clap on her thighs.

I want to be amused by her small outburst. The wrinkle in her brow and slight scrunch of the nose now familiar to me.

Before when I had run into her, or confused her during our planning session, I thought her frustration was at me specifically. Now I am seeing she needs to find control in an uncontrolled situation. She wants to clean, organize, and plan because that's what makes her raft float at a steadier pace.

The confliction that crosses her face as she eyes my bare chest makes my smile grow.

"Can't I convince you to come back to bed?" I ask, already feeling my cock firming. The tenting of the sheets around my groin doesn't go unnoticed.

"But we just did," she waves her hand towards me, "that."

Her shyness to name the dirty actions— the ones we have just finished— makes me laugh. "Did what, Elle?" I shuffle to the edge of the bed, letting the sheet fall away. Her breath hitches, and my confidence balloons in my chest. I grip her wrists, pulling her back towards the edge of the mattress.

"I know you have a filthy mouth." I say pressing my lips to the inside of each of her wrists. Blue irises trace the movement, as my head turns and repeats the action further up her arms.

"But we just fucked," she whispers, her breath hitching again as my lips meet the skin on the inside of her right elbow. I drag my tongue across the feathersoft skin, allowing my hand to lift the soft cotton hem of her shirt. Before digging my fingers into her hips.

"Are you telling me you can't go another rou–" before I finish speaking, her hands are pulling from my grasp and she slowly lifts her shirt up, up, up, up, until her breasts reveal themselves. Nipples are perfectly pink and hard. Begging for my attention, making my mouth suddenly dry.

She tangles the shirt over her head, her bob of brown hair falling over her brows as she flings it aside.

"Gorgeous." I say, unsure why all vocabulary has vanquished my brain. "Perfect."

She laughs at the sweet sound that is my siren call, the one I would follow over a cliff. The woman who was truly made in heaven, just for me.

Perfectly framed legs bend as she climbs back onto the mattress. Before I remember how to breathe her leg vaults over my torso as she crawls on top of me. The look on my face must be humorous, because a delicate giggle escapes her as she settles further onto my torso. I am immediately hard as stone from the sound, the action, the sanctuary I never want to leave.

Her hips swivel, lining us up against each other, and causing my cock to jump at the sensation of her warmth grazing the head. My heart pounds incredibly loud in my chest, the thump reverberating in my ears. I grip her ass with eager hands, and thankfully some grace. Now that the unfamiliarity between us has completely faded, our bodies connect like magnets.

The second we touch, our atoms fizz alive with energy, encouraging us to be nowhere but fully pressed together. Hair falls around my face as I look up to meet her gaze. Her eyes close and she tips her forehead to mine.

"Please tell me that this is real?" she whispers. The breath off her lips dancing across my nose.

"Elle," I breathe, and her blue eyelids fly open to meet my gaze. In a brief moment of uncertainty I look at her mouth.

The breath she takes is all in preparation for the worst, she's preparing for the reason for us not to do this again. The first time, a fling, a quick one night stand. Twice would cement something in her, and in me. I know this because I normally leave. I don't let women believe the cuddling thing is on the table. I stop myself before it ever gets too much, or too strong, because I am broken. I have been since I left home at eighteen. Honestly since the death of my mom.

But with Elle, I feel like my cup is refilling, overflowing, being washed off all the muck and mud until the liquid runs clear.

Leaving Elle seems impossible at this moment. Ever truly. Imagining her with anyone else seems ridiculous. The idea is scary as hell, if I am being honest, and will definitely scare her too. As the idea swims across my brain, all I can see is her blue eyes full of wonder.

She wants this, even if it's for now. I realize now is what I want to hold onto, so I flatten my palms on her lower back. Brushing my palms against the soft skin on her lower back.

"Tell me you feel this," I whisper, pulling her warm breast so they're pressed further onto my chest. Her chin dips and our lips brush briefly. "Feel how real this is."

"I feel like you're definitely hard," she jokes.

My hands find her jaw, tugging until her lips meet mine again. "Wait, we need a condom."

"It's fine." she says, kissing the corner of my mouth as she does.

"Are you sure, Your Highness?"

"I'm on the pill." She says, as her hips wriggle over my groin again, sliding her wet core over the head of my dick.

"Now you say that?" and I thrust up, and my heart threatens to explode at the feeling of the tip of my dick inching inside her. "I'm clean." I say on the back of a breath, my fingers digging harder into her thighs to hold her up. I have to wait, but she's making it so damn impossible.

"Me too." Her blue irises search my face, before she shakes her head "I'm sorry, I've never done it without a condom."

My hands release their grip on her thighs, finding the curve of her chin instead, I brush the hair from her face, tilting her face gently until her eyes meet mine. "Don't apologize. You never have to apologize for something like that."

She doesn't respond, but her body weight shifts and my dick is immediately engulfed by her. A small gasp escapes her as she takes every inch of my bare shaft to the hilt with ease.

This. This feeling, the closest we could be. Every wall she has eradicated falling away, every inch of her skin touching mine. Everything about this round of entanglements is familiar, trusting, even the roll of her hips and the urge to speed things up simply... fades away.

I want to bottle up this moment between us so I can drink from it whenever I need to. My tongue guides her lips open and the taste of her. Her arms wrap around my neck as I find her nipple with my mouth, and the moan she releases is feral. She's pressing fingers into my shoulders, into the headboard with the other— all in an effort to steady herself. She guides herself up and down slowly, squeezing my cock as she takes it in fully. Kisses my cheeks, my forehead, and then the very tip of my nose. Making it incredibly hard for me to not burst at her carnivores' needs.

She unfolds, giving me the glorious view of her tits bouncing as I thrust up, and her hips circle. Her hands find her center and her eyelids fall closed. Her mouth forms the perfect O and if I thought I was a goner before, I am deceased now. She was so unbelievably beautiful naturally, but intoxicating with me buried deep inside her. My nerves jump at the urge to move out of this position before it becomes too hard to refrain.

My hands find her thighs and lift us until her back meets the soft billowing sheets under us. I drive into her with a few thrusts, her hips meeting my every movement.

"Fuck," she moans as I kiss her chin, her cheeks, then I trail more down her neck.

"Don't stop talking," I say, begging to hear her voice again. Wanting the filthy things she says to come out again.

"What should I say?" Her hands find the hair at the nape of my neck and her fingers grip the ends tight in her knuckles. I thrust into her at a slow steady pace.

"Whatever you want to," I say, and when she doesn't immediately respond I pull back to meet her gaze again—baby blue irises glistening and set on me. Her short brown hair is fanned out around her like a halo and as her swollen lips are sucked in by her teeth my chest tightens. I love how beautiful she is. I *love* her. I love *her.*

My heart trips over a metaphorical barrier and I am falling hard for Elizabeth O'Hare as I am driving my cock so deep inside her. The realization is heavy and I shift the weight onto my elbows. Pressing them into the mattress and my forehead finds the groove of her neck.

I don't stop thrusting. Afraid if I do I'll lose this— lose her. That she'll dwindle away. That I'll fall from this grace and crash onto the pavement.

"Tell me what you want, Your Highness." I breath into her ear, closing my eyes and breathing the scent of her shampoo.

Vanilla.

It's simple but, like her, it's warm and consistent. The scent that never fades or becomes overbearing. The kind that wafts to you when you need a warm hug or a cookie hot from the oven. Elle is just like vanilla I realize— always there, always perfect in her own way, always beautiful.

"I want you, Devin." She says, her voice unwavering. I want her too, so badly that I am afraid of my next words so I groan in response.

I thrust into her deeper, her knee brushes my hip bone and I curl my arm through its loop, stretching her further.

Then when she trembles beneath me, beckons me with her pants to follow her over the edge. I think of dirty socks, dead cats, and quite porcelain bathrooms. Any attempt to hold out for her to come more times than me.

Which she does, three more times before I can't hold it any longer.

"That's so hot." I groan after she settles from her last climax. We are a mess of sweat and heavy breaths, and I have never felt so exhilarated.

"Come for me." She begs, and her hand lowers to my ass, fingers digging into the flesh as she does anything and everything to fortify us closer. I drive into her, watching her face contort with pleasure and I don't think I can hold onto my composure any longer.

If I come this will end, I'm too exhausted not to fight off the lethargy after, I already know it.

"Come inside me," she says on the precipice of a whisper, and I slow my hip's rhythm.

"Elle," my gaze finds hers again as she wriggles beneath me, "say it again."

"Devin," she plants a quick kiss to my mouth, "I want all of you."

I groan and my forehead falls to hers. Never in all my life have I ever come inside a woman bare. I never wanted to, not until now. There was nothing I've ever wanted more than to come inside of Elle right now. Fill her up, feel her clamp around me, pump me dry, all while I finally meet the height of my ecstasy.

"Come for me." She says into my ear, her breath's heat and the words she is saying lighting me on fire. I'm on the edge, and my thrusting picks up. I release everything–

every ounce of restraint. Three words teetering on the edge of my brain as my muscles go rigid and she relaxes underneath me. I can't move, and I want to pass out right here.

The next moments are fuzzy, she's asking to get up, to leave my embrace, but I don't want that. I need to get up, help her clean up, then I can sleep.

Surprised that I have any strength to rise, I retrieve a white towel from the ensuite bathroom, and whip the space between her legs clean. Flopping onto the mattress face first, and the cotton instantly relaxes me. I sense her absence briefly, hear the toilet flush, and peek an eye open to watch her tug on a pair of underwear and a tee shirt. Her tired eyes find me and she says one single phrase that I didn't know I was hoping for, "So you're staying."

I smile, because out of context that would seem like a questioning phrase, a dig, or even a sarcastic comment. Elle seems frosty if you listen to the words alone, but I hear the optimism in her voice, it's faint but there all the same. I groan and she folds onto the bed, and I wrap my arm around her warm torso tugging her back to my chest, wrapping so tight around her. Falling so deep into sleep I don't dream at all.

Chapter Sixteen

Saturday

ELLE

P anic.

Panic is the only reasonable response to waking to find a very attractive Devin sprawled on my bed. His gloriously muscled back on full display. Adorned in little tattoos that all seem to be misplaced, yet all most likely were chosen for a very specific reason. I notice flora, script, tiny shapes—some solid black, others outlines. My eyes linger on the 22 peeking out from his side, only the edge visible, but the lines look the fuzziest. It's his oldest looking one.

Devin— whimsy as he is— has made himself more than comfortable in my bed after a long night of the best sex I have ever had. Finding it more than suitable to make himself right at home in my apartment is making me a little uneasy. The very heavy fact that I let him come inside me also weighing me down.

I shuffle out from under his arm, making sure that he grips my pillow instead. He rolls onto his side with a groan, but doesn't seem to wake.

Memories of his soft touches and many kisses follow me into my small bathroom. He said things. I said *things*. We didn't say anything too deep, yet I felt completely exposed.

The sight of my frazzled bob of brown hair, and smeared mascara are making it hard to overlook that I simply can not, and will not, get used to this.

He does this with every girl he finds attractive, I tell myself. Even though the idea that he may find me attractive does lift my spirits slightly, he is still a fraternity man. Therefore being seen as a "chill one night stand" in his eyes is the approach I must go with. This wasn't a one night stand, was it? He told me he wanted me. To solely date me.

I begin my extensive skin care routine, hoping the cold water washes away the slight shame I am beginning to feel. Then cleansing my compulsiveness with mad foaming circles. Next is toner, hopefully tightening up my pores and my panic into something positive. Then Vitamin C Serum for extra positivity. Add in some spot corrector on a few blemishes— ones that I am convinced just formed due to the stress. Before I finish with my favorite moisturizing sunscreen.

Silence greets me as I tilt my ear to the door, hoping to not have woken Devin yet.

I hear nothing, so I gently turn the handle and press on the door with my palm until I am peaking out into the faintly lit bedroom.

My hands fall to my sides at the realization that the bed is not only empty, but it's made. My floral comforter has been neatly placed back over the sheets, folded to the top neatly and the pillows— including the ones I use for decoration— are neatly thrown atop. The curtains have been opened— explaining the light now in the room— and the scent of coffee is coming through the slightly ajar door leading from the main living area. I tip toe over to my door and peer out through the crack between the hinges. I can't see Devin but I can hear him rummaging about in the cabinets. Closing them with small thuds as he searches for something.

"You didn't leave?" I ask, tugging at the hem of the shirt I am wearing, like I am trying to cover myself.

I realize I am doing so because he will most likely storm into my room again. Confidently too, like he does in every room. I also move away from my hiding place in case that exact occurrence happens and I don't want to relive the past by getting run over. I feel silly for forgetting that he has already seen me naked. Been inside me.

"Was I supposed to?" His voice is giddy— like always— but the thudding doesn't stop.

"What are you looking for?" I say, gently closing the door so I can reach my dresser and find some pants.

"Um." He pauses, then says, "do you have a slotted spatula?"

"A what?" I reach the dresser and pull at the top drawer, finding my four neat piles in matching baskets of underwear and bras. One for when I'm on my period— you know "grandma looking"— then reach for the second stack. They are pairs I purchased "just incase" and now I am realizing that it's the exact case now. Not that I think Devin will see them, but secretly I'm kind of hoping he will. Then I grab a sports bra out of one of the bra piles.

"Like a spatula for flipping things." His voice cuts through my distress.

"Flipping things?" I squeak, tossing my old pair of garments into the bin next to the dresser.

"Yeah," he laughs, like for pancakes."

"You're making me pancakes?" I say, pushing my head and shoulder through the sports bra holes and tugging aggressively to get it situated in place.

"It was going to be a surprise but–"

"I'm surprised." I yell, my voice coming out loud and awkward.

I take an absurdly large breath and pull out the remainder of my clothes. I slip into a pair of black sport shorts, loose and comfortable. Topped with a light green crew neck that has Kappa Sigma Iota scribbled in a pink cursive font delicately across the chest.

Today, I technically don't have anything I need to be doing for the sorority, but I know that if I don't at least check my emails, I'll regret it.

I do one more once over in the mirror on the back of my door before swinging it wide and walking out.

Devin's blonde crown is all I can see over the counter top, and he doesn't seem to notice I have entered the main living area until I round the counter.

"What are you looking for?" I ask, my eyes catching on the full sink of dishes, the bowl of white pancake batter next to it with a spoon resting on the edge, batter dripping onto the counter. Then to the stove top where one of my only pans is smoking slightly.

"A spatula for the–" his hazel eyes trail up my bare legs. From where he's crouched, there is little doubt that he can see up my shorts, so I shift my legs over one another.

"Under the sink?" I say, trying to ignore the giant mess in my small kitchen.

"Well," he stands to his full height, and I tilt my head to meet his gaze, "you're so organized everywhere else that I assumed I could find everything, but now I'm convinced you don't own a spatula at all." His smile is all teeth and the dimples I have come well acquainted with start to show.

"I don't cook much." I say, glancing at the smoking stove again.

He quickly removes the pan from the red ringed top and places it on the cool side.

"That's okay," he says, no concern for the half batter half cooked pancake that sits in the pan, "I don't mind."

I step to move around him, the tight quarters forcing us to brush chests as I go. Quickly, I turn to tug on a drawer next to the fridge.

"Does this work?" I ask, holding up a small wood handle tool with a flimsy pink plastic head.

"I'll make it work." His voice is close to my ear, and before I turn his arms are wrapping around my waist and spinning me to him. Every nerve ending in my body boils at the touch. I'm not sure what the hell is happening and I have the faint nag to ask. But then another small part of me says, *this is what happens after you fuck the hot man who made you dinner on the first date,* and *he feels like he has to make breakfast too because you let him stay.*

"Great, because I am starving," are the embarrassing words that actually fly from my mouth.

His hand lifts to grip my chin and the breath I release is all instinctual. I am thrown right back into the hot and heavy moments when this apartment was dark.

"Thank you," his breath dances across my lips and his fingers clasp around the spatula. Brushing mine, and causing another bolt of lightning to rush through me. I tilt my head up and our noses touch. He brushes a feather light kiss on the tip of my nose and my lids fall close. Realizing I love when he does that.

My inner dialogue chants at me to calm down.

This is just infatuation. Just him being nice. Just hot men, doing hot things. Don't get to attached Elle.

I squeeze my core and my legs shift, causing me to fall away from our closeness, he clears his throat and backs away.

"You are very distracting." He says as he turns away, and I am reminded that he is calm and collected because this is *chill*. So I therefore need to calm the hell down and be fucking chill.

"Sorry," I breath and duck my head, quickly shuffling out of the kitchen and finding my laptop in the living room.

I set it up on the counter and pretend that it is open to my email, while in all actuality I watch Devin continue making breakfast.

Making *me* breakfast.

Devin's making me breakfast.

I realize then and there, while he flips perfectly round pancakes, feeds them to me on a plate, and drizzles them in syrup that he bought the night before, that I am completely fucked.

I am fucked because I have not only fucked a fraternity man, now I am falling for Sigma Rho Beta man.

I'm falling hard. Is what I think.

"Fuck," is what I say, when the first bite of fluffy pancakes hits my tongue.

Chapter Seventeen

Saturday

DEVIN

My dorm room is as gross as I remembered. Between running to the store for all the food that I bought to make Elle dinner and breakfast— before coming back to shower and shave— my apartment was left in what looks like the aftermath of a tornado.

Literally, I think there are clothes hanging on every surface, and normally I wouldn't mind but when Elle asked to come up my anxiety spiked and I told her to stay. That it would be quick, no need to make her leave the warm car. I could've sworn that I picked up— at least made my bed— but this place is nowhere as clean as Elle's.

So now I am throwing more clothes around in an attempt to quickly find a clean shirt and pants. I lift a black pair of shorts that I wore a few days ago to my face, and sniff the fabric.

"Fuck, no," I grumble to myself, tossing the garment aside.

I'm not sure where I am going to take her now, just that when I suggested we do something that she grew a look of pure shook, overlapping her otherwise flat appearance. Making me want to do something to keep her smiling. Also talking, we conversed so much over breakfast, reaffirming I don't ever want her to stop talking.

Covering all the topics, favorite colors (Hers: Green; Mine: Black), what our favorite movie genres were (Hers: Romcom; Mine: Also Romcom but in an attempt to seem "cool" I said Thriller).

I had a very long mental list of things I wanted to know about her, but I needed to hurry the fuck up before she left, or worse came into this fucking disgusting excuse of a dorm room.

I find a white tee shirt in the back of my wardrobe, and a pair of jeans that are draped over the towel rail in the bathroom. Shoving my limbs into them with rapt intent.

By the time I climb into the cab of Elle's SUV she's already had time to pull out her laptop— one I didn't know she brought. Along with her phone that is beaming a hot spot.

I hear a voice come through the miniature speaker of the device, and Elle presses a finger to her lips encouraging my silence.

"I'll need to talk to our regional advisor, but I think it needs to be handled before the Judicial Board hearings tomorrow afternoon."

Elle doesn't respond, simply shifts the laptop around the steering wheel to more easily type on her keyboard. I shift in silently— watching her with furrowed brows— unsure if she is in some sort of trouble. I have never seen her in a state of worry this tense before. I still know very little about Greek life, but I do know being asked to attend our Judicial meetings is not a positive event.

"I have already been working with Shannon regarding how to handle it, but I think you should also sit in." Elle stares at the space between her seat and the center console, "at least with the meeting beforehand to prepare."

"Okay," she says, her tone firm, "I can do that, Thank you Leah."

Leah says her parting words, then hangs up. I'm not sure how to fill the silent tension in the small space, so I simply grab her hand as it retracts from her phone.

She shakes her head, closes her laptop and faces me. The smile she directs towards me is small, and far too ingenuine for my liking.

"What's wrong?" I say, rubbing circles over the back of her hand. The soft skin pebbles with goose flesh and she grips tighter.

"Nothing, just something with the chapter," she says again and her voice is small, "something I have to deal with tomorrow.

Fires.

Trent had told me that fires are what he has to deal with the most as a president. I wasn't sure what he meant then, but it seemed that Elle was currently filling buckets of water to pour out a fire she didn't really want to deal with. The weight of that was overwhelming to me.

"What can I do to help?" I say, unsure if there is a single thing to fix a problem I know nothing about.

"Can we go see a movie?" She says, turning her blue irises to me.

"Sure." She pulls her hand from mine and starts the ignition, "Do you want to talk about it?"

"It's not really something I can talk about." She's back to her direct self, it's an honest answer and if we weren't more familiar now, I could see how people would conceive her responses as cold.

She doesn't mean to be monosyllable, much like myself, "I get that." I say and she glances my way as she backs out of the parking spot.

I drum my fingers on the door handle, hoping she will speak without me having to ask. I want to so desperately tell her about what happened at U of C but only a few people know the entire story. I don't think she needs the weight of knowing what I did added to her stress.

I can hardly bear the stress and guilt of it most days. Having dreamt about it so often, waking with a tight chest and the urge to scream or cry. Dreams too realistic for my heart to handle— seeing the girl tipped out of the bathtub, arms limp. The screams of her friend when they barreled in the small powder room. Cocaine still in neat little piles along the counter, the itch in my nostrils from having just snorted some myself before I noticed her presence. Being so thrilled one moment about free drugs, then scared by her lifeless eyes the next.

I had experienced death, but never first hand like that. My mom was simply with us some days then "on vacation" others. After one of the times away, I think this time had been a week, I couldn't remember for certain. All I remember is we watched movies all day— mostly classics, her favorites— Funny Face, Casablanca, Breakfast at Tiffany's. Built a fort with the couch cushions, and she made snacks of all kinds. Popcorns with various flavoring sweet and salty, five or six batches of cookies, and microwave nachos. You know the kind with the cheap tortilla chips and bright orange cheddar shredders—cooked until the entire clump sticks to the paper plate. I even remember the final kiss she placed on the tip of my nose when I finally collapsed onto my Star Wars themed twin bed. Then a few days later, my dad picked me up from school right after recess, and told me she was gone.

"Where'd you go?" Elle asks, and I startle. I let myself think about that night and the last true quality time with my mom— instead of remaining present and I hate that I did.

"Ah," I clear my throat and adjust the temperature heater, decreasing the fan slightly, "No where." I say, plastering on a huge grin.

"Good," she says and I am instantly reminded of what I want to be present for right now. That *now* is all that matters. Elle is all that matters, because she needs me to at least distract her for today. Help reaffirm her smile even if it's just for today.

I reach for her thigh, resting my hand on the soft warm fabric of her leggings. This pair is dark green and topped with a light gray crew neck. She has a lot of versions of the same outfit, not much unlike myself. Perpetually comfy and confident about it. I think I like that the most about her. She's authentically herself, and I realize I like her just the way she is. I told her as much last night but we haven't discussed it much after that.

"What date is this?" I ask, gripping her thigh with a gentle squeeze.

"I don't know, you tell me."

"I think it's three."

"It's only been forty-eight hours since our first," she huffs. "How could it be three?"

"Well I made you dinner, and you fucked my face." My blunt statement makes her cheeks redden, and she scoffs at me— only making me laugh. "Then there was the snack run, and I fucked your face."

"Devin!" she chastises, and swats her hand at my shoulder. I catch her wrist and firmly kiss the back of it before she pulls away.

"You're distracting me." She says, as we pull up to a redlight.

"Good, now you know how it feels," I take this as an opportunity to make her squirm more, "and we have fucked three times."

"Twice." She amends and then proceeds to turn us left through the green glowing light.

"I think you are forgetting the shower this morning."

"Oh yeah," she giggles, "probably because it wasn't very memorable."

Her joke makes my entire body shake as I laugh and I grip the inside of her thigh again, making her squeal my name. She's trying—with a steel spine— not to be distracted by me while she drives and I love making her feel out of control. Seeing her ribbons unravel for me and reveal the gift underneath all her neatly wrapped foil.

I decide to leave it at that, and look out at the mountain towering over us as we drive along them, grazing the base as the frontage road winds close to them. Colorado is gorgeous this time of year, yellow leaves flying off the white Aspens as their spotted trunks sway in the wind. And at that moment, in all her gloriousness I never felt like I ever really missed it when I was in Cali. Never had anyone but a Jinny to miss here.

I glance at my phone, unsure what to expect other than the photo of Elle and I from last night. We had made them our screensavers at my suggestion. Even though she thought I was joking I made a point to show her it was still there whenever I could. In all honesty I wanted to look at it, her beautiful blue eyes murdering the lens with their hue and her soft pouty lips smiling slightly as her chin rested on my shoulder. Our faces took up the entire screen, but all I saw was *her*.

Elle turns the radio up and as Dylan Scott's baritone voice sings My Girl through the speakers, I am washed with the realization that I want to stay.

Chapter Eighteen

Saturday

ELLE

I stare at the tiny phone screen in front of me. Laura's voice murmurs in my ears, I can't fathom what I am seeing. Can't stop the pounding in my ears enough to hear what she is saying fully. The words "branding" and "Sigma Rho Beta Brothers" and "contract" are the few things I manage to grasp.

"What sisters?" I ask, afraid and curious all in one moment that I can't quite bottle.

No one responds at first and I can feel my veins ready to pop. My eyes slam shut and I hear Shannons answer. "Dani and Kelly."

Dani is the curve ball, she's one of the nicest girls in the chapter. Then there's Kelly, my little.

Each of us was given the opportunity to mentor and welcome a sister into the chapter. Shower them with gifts as a new member and teach them the ways of the lifestyle. Kelly was one of three of *my* little sisters. So the reality of this all really drives the dagger straight into my heart. As president, I am overly busy, and expected to be impartial all of the time so I know I am not a wonderful big sister. I am not one who is able to spend copious amounts of time with them— nor would I truly know how. Plus they had each other now, and their own friends from their recruitment classes.

I'm idolized but I know they saw me for what I am— their president. The same role of a parent, and in college you're prone to rebel. So I wasn't intune to what they all did, but they all got along— we even took the "family" photos— but now I was realizing I truly was failing them. Especially Kelly, but maybe all of them, but most of all her. She has always been the mustang, wild and beautifully free. Young but already showing so much dedication to the chapter and now I am unsure of her future standing in the chapter.

"Why would they do this?" I ask, finally able to tear my eyes from the screen and meet the matching sullen expressions that Laura and Leah are giving me. Next to me Shannon shifts, brushing her black hair behind her ear, before she flicks the screen to the next photo.

"They signed a contract." She says, and my mouth falls open. "Stating they would be Sigma Rho Beta *little sisters*."

"That's not a thing," I gasp. "Is that that a thing?" I direct the question at Leah. I think I want to cry, but I am in shock. I have never been in shock, but I imagine the lack of complete control plus the delayed sense of panic is just that.

She draws in a deep breath and observes the three of us— not much younger than she is, yet all of us are being thrown into something much larger than many adults ever face.

"In some Greek cultures yes, but it's an outdated concept." She pauses and the room falls silent again. The usual faint hum of the fluorescents above don't bring us any comfort. "But KSI headquarters wants us to present it as hazing."

Sisters that make up the Judicial Board are lining up outside the door. Sisters that will need to call the girls in that were branded.

I look at the images again, blistered skin, all interconnecting in furious red lines over otherwise clean shoulder blades. Shoulder blades of girls I was meant to protect. Now they are forever branded with the SRB letters. Furthermore these girls will be reporting to the judicial board, then possibly the University. All under a story that seems so muddled with fantasy and drunken endeavors now being flipped, and the words *Hazing*, and

Branded will be stamped with Kappa Sigma Iota's name in the reports handed to Holden.

"Does Holden know?" I ask, panic rising in my voice.

Leah reacts like I slapped her, then straightens her spine, "Not yet, but Shannon will need to report SRB, in hopes of finding out who did this. So he will find out soon."

It's illegal to haze in Colorado— I know that at the least. What that will mean for all the members of Greek life involved with this I am not certain.

"What Brothers? How do you have these photos?"

"They were posted on Zapchat and someone sent them directly to me," Shannon pipes up, "under a false email."

"And we don't know which brothers, just that it happened sometime on Friday night," adds Leah.

Slight relief floods into me— Devin was with me that night. Hadn't he mentioned some party? I start racking my brain for more explanations, but I realize quickly it won't change anything.

My birthday is this week. That thought intrudes into my head and I can't believe that before I am even legally able to drink I am confronted with the thought of the pain that one must endure when being branded like cattle. Then the anger that follows suit from the fact that members younger than myself were with men that allowed this to occur.

"We just wanted to inform you, obviously we didn't need you hearing about this from someone else?" Laura's voice is calm and collected, but I have known her since we joined the chapter together. She doesn't want to be dealing with this, even if she has the slightest idea what to do. It's more likely that none of us do.

"We'll let you know how the trials go." Leah states, and I am flushed back with the reality that I can't do anything about this. My hands are tied, and my lips need to be sealed.

"Okay," I say, lifting from my seat. My limbs feel phantom and wobbly. I manage to make it to the door without crumbling and I fling open the door. Faced with the sight of so many soft and innocent faces. I expect to see Kelly, but she most likely has been given a specific time to show up for her trial.

Each sister gives me a soft smile, then shuffles in around me as I hold open the door. Some of them must know what happened, but others will be as taken back as I was.

The hall becomes empty— aside from my own presence— and I feel it. Heavy responsibility bracketing my shoulders, like Atlas hoisting up the globe.

I make my way down the hall and into the room where we host a formal meeting. We have about an hour until our start time, but the room is already set up in our meeting arrangement. The universities's Event Department is incharge of all that.

So I fold myself into my seat at the center of the table and gaze out over the rows of chairs facing it. No one prepares you fully for the strength it takes to sit in the center of the room every week— demanding attention. All while steering the train back on the rails, rails that are flimsy and fragile. That breaks at the slightest inconvenience and the destination is forever unknown.

I let my arms fall to the table and I tuck my head into them. Urging myself to cry, and begging the tears to fall for my sisters. For my chapter's fate.

Anything.

But no tears fall, no panic sets in. Instead I am stuck in a state of shock, realizing I most likely was already there a while ago. Numb to the surprises. Always expecting the worst. My parents divorce, failing school, and running a chapter that is in a constant state of hidden chaos.

The door slams open and a few members of my executive board flood in around me, I raise my head and Frankie's halo of red hair is the first thing I see. She's carrying robes and chatting at the speed of light, obviously unaware of everything happening in the room down the hall.

"You alright?" Hillary asks, attempting to place a black cloth across the table that I am leaning on.

"Yeah," I say, forcing myself to seem normal, "I'm fine."

She eyes me for a brief moment then says, "Okay," before reaching into her bag and pulling out candles and setting them in front of me. Another brief glance occurs between us, then she places my gavel in front of me.

She leaves me to sit and collect my thoughts, and I am not sure how long I sit there as the rest of the board flutters around me. It is only until I realize I am gripping my gavel so tight in my fist that I take a deep steadying breath. Slamming this thing— even if it's just to start the meeting— will feel very cathartic today.

Chapter Nineteen

Sunday

DEVIN

M ile's is packed full with all the Sigma Rho Beta brothers— dressed in slacks and button up shirts. All of various shades of neutrals, some even paired with decorative ties and matching pocket squares. After our formal meeting we always end up all huddled around the small circle tables or sprinkled over the small rectangle ones— completely monopolizing the space.

"And that's why I drafted him as the first pick, but now I am unsure if he'll play." Brooks states, pointing towards the television, that the small circle of us are gathered below in the corner. He's flailing his palms in the air— aiming them at the screen— while Geoff nods seemingly following along with what he is saying. Clearly understanding more than I do about the topic. I know they are discussing fantasy football drafts, but I don't care.

I have my book in my hand, but the thought of opening it while the rest of them stand around me feels weird. So

I pretend to know and nod, gaze at the green field on the screen then sip my beer.

Trent saunters in the door, and he searches the crowd until his eyes catch on mine. I nod and he waves a hand in a gesture I am assuming means he wants me to come to him. I hesitate briefly, not wanting to be rude. Before I decide on my better judgement and excuse myself— no one seems to notice. RJ just fills my spot, to get a better view and he assimulates himself seamlessly into the conversation that I just departed.

It takes me a few moments to get through the crowd, lifting my beer away from swinging elbows and jumping shoulders. A few brothers clap my shoulders as I pass and I tip my head with a smile each time.

"Devin, perfect." Trent says, like we happened to run into one another. Not that he summoned me. "I need to chat with you."

I agree and he angles us towards the bar, I gesture at the tender for another pint as I slam back the rest of the bronze liquid in my glass. Trent orders the same and we wait in thick silence while the bars tender tugs on the spouts on the back wall.

Trent checks his phone, huffing as he clicks it closed then shoves it into the inside of his jacket— because yes he is wearing a four piece suit. Vest and all, matching in a glorious crimson color. His black tie is speckled with tiny golden SRB letters, clasped together with a shiny engraved pin with the word *president* on it.

"Nice tie clip," I say.

He doesn't seem to have heard me until he stammers out, "What? Oh this old thing, Thanks."

"What's up Trent?"

"Are you going home for winter break?" He says, as our beers are set in front of us.

"That's what you wanted to ask me?"

"No. Well," he turns towards the crowd of brothers at our back, before slicing his gaze back to me. "I was just curious."

He seems off— there's no other way to label it.

I decide to ignore it, instead I say, "No, Jinny's coming and I am showing her around campus."

"Oh right, J graduates soon." He nods, and his lips roll together. "I didn't know she was coming to Conifer Valley next fall."

"I think it'll be in January."

"Sounds like her." He rolls his brown eyes, and glaces over my shoulder.

"Are you okay?"

"Yeah, yeah, yeah," he chants with a huffed laugh. "I actually was wanting to hear if you convinced Elle, yet?"

I hadn't even thought about what Trent had asked of me regarding Elle. There was no way he knew I was with her all weekend, or that I had basically come right from her place to the chapter's meeting.

I clear my throat, "I haven't really seen her much."

"But the social event was planned?" Trent says, before sipping the foam off the top of his glass.

"Yeah, of course," I shrug, faking nonchalance.

"So you're seeing her then."

I choke on my beer, spewing it towards Trent and he backs away in disgust.

"Putain, man?" He swipes at the front of his jacket with a small black square napkin.

"Sorry," I huff, holding back a laugh, "wrong pipe." Nothing about this is funny, Trent's reaction was just so juvenile. He looks like a toddler dressed up in a suit, his dark black hair falling from the slicked gelled wave keeping it in place— so now the image is making me want to die of laughter. Elle would laugh for sure.

"The Greek space did not come up." I say, swiping another napkin off the bar and handing it to him.

He snatches it away and I catch him glaring at a few of the brothers near us as they stare.

"Well we have about a week."

"A Week."

"Yes, a week until Holden wants us to take a vote. I convinced him to move it up. Told him it is important that I, as well as my members, focus solely on finals before break." He explains, his voice filled with slight annoyance.

"Okay."

"Perfect, then I'll add you to the group chat for that committee." He says, swiping his phone open and typing frantically. "Ren's in charge, but I told him I'd talk to you."

"What?" I say beer sloshes over the rim of my glass as I move instinctually.

Trents jaw tightened as the liquid barrels to the floor next to his shiny black loafers. "Bro, these are Hermès," he says, thick with an accent. I know Trent well enough to understand that he isn't joking.

"Sorry," I grumble.

My phone buzzes in my pocket but I don't dare to remove it, trepidation floods in at the idea of Trent seeing the photo of Elle and I together. I don't know if he'll care, he'll most likely be overjoyed. Stating it's "great for greek life" or whatever he had insinuated less than a week ago.

Everything with Elle was new and raw. So fresh that I didn't want to share it with anyone just yet, other than Jinny. I had told her immediately on the phone outside the gas station. Her squeals most likely carried out the speaker and back to the car.

Elle was still in the meeting, but most likely had just closed— if that was even her texting. It isn't worth the risk, so I ignore it. Trent is glancing around the bar again, seemingly done with me.

"Are you going home for the break?" I ask, unsure where our friendship lines are. We have always been transparent but never really sharing the emotional stuff.

"No, I have to take a winter class, " he shrugs.

"Oh which one?"

"Some English Lit. class, I don't want to take it for a full term so I am getting it over with."

"Oh smart."

"What about you?" he shakes the hands of a few brothers who are leaving the bar, "are you taking any classes since you'll be here?"

"Depends on how finals go I guess."

"Yeah, well," he taps the cover of my book as it rests on the bar next to me, "you've always been really smart."

"Yeah, I'm not worried."

I toss back the remainder of my beer and Trent sips on his almost full glass. I need to go— if I drink any more I won't be able to make the drive over to Elle's place.

"I gotta head out, man." I say, cupping Trent's hand as he stretches it out to me. We conduct the hand shake and then I am practically jumping out the door and pulling out my phone.

"Tell Jinny hi for me." He yells after me, and I am a bit confused how they actually know each other.

The first thing I see is a text from Jinny, which is a weird coincidence, but then I see it's over the photo of Elle. Both sights bring a smile to my lips.

Jinny: Blair and Dan are now a thing!!! Sorry to Spoil it! I can't hold in my anger!

i told you i'm not going to watch it.

also trent says hi

Jinny: Who's Trent?

trent turner

I swipe over to the list of messages and send off a text to Elle. I type it once, then retype it with proper grammar before hitting send.

When can I see you? Tonight?

She doesn't respond right away, so I swipe back over to Jinny's message, avoiding a few people in the hall as I aim towards the back doors leading to the dorms.

Jinny: EW, well, I am gonna drive down on Friday, does that still work? Or is Elle staying in your dorm?

I'm gonna try to stay at her place, so you can have my room to yourself

Jinny: EW. But also adorable.

i gotta go

Jinny: Tell her I say hi, and tell Trent to shove his BMW key up his ass.

I laugh, as a message from Elle flashes across the top of the screen and I am instantly disappointed.

Her Royal Highness: Can't tonight, still in meetings. Still good for Tuesday?

of course

Her Royal Highness: Good night, Devin.

good night, your highness

Chapter Twenty

Tuesday

ELLE

The Conifer Valley Zoo is sparkling in its holiday colors. The light festival being one of the most notorious of its events, bedazzling the space with tiny bulbed lights in all the festive shades. The typical greens and reds of Christmas are used to fill most of the trees, but all the colors imaginable outline other images of wild animals. Some cast the illusion of running or jumping species, while some wrap around already constructed life size sculptures.

The "feeding the zebras" exhibit is usually the only spectacle at the zoo but now both attractions lead to the enormous crowd that surrounds us. Normally the amount of people crowded around the fences— with their gloved hands gripping the chain links like the animals were going to jump out at any moment— would have bothered me, but there is something about Devin's excitement, mostly the way he clings to my hand, that is making it hard to identify any issues with the night.

"Have you ever been here before?" Devin asks, his excitement painted across his face with his infamous smile, his dimples blaring cherry red in the cold.

"A couple times." I reply, and a small streak of disappointment flashes across his features, "but never for the holiday lights festival."

I follow Devin as he guides us to leave the feeding area, through the other sleeping exhibits, and under a tunnel of white lights leading to the house of aquatic animals.

"I didn't really like fish." I blurt at the sight of brass aquatic animals decorating the outside of the building.

"I think there are penguins in here," Devin gestures a thumb over his shoulder— tugging on my hand slightly as I force us to stop in our tracks. "You can close your eyes, and I'll guide you through, if that helps?"

"I nod, closing my eyes, instinctively stepping closer to him. Our jackets rub together and the sound brings me comfort. I am about to explode, until Devin wraps an arm around my waist and the contact of his hand tucked into the back pocket of my jeans is all I can focus on. The warmth and graze of his firm hands sends a tingle up my spine and my mouth falls open.

I refuse to open my eyes, because the air around us is warm so I know we're inside. We have moved past the entry to the building, I can feel Devin shifting around me to open doors. He is saying a few words of thanks to strangers around us. Most likely for moving out of the way of the scared girl.

I'm very aware that his hand never leaves the pocket, because his palm is wrapped around my left ass cheek. This attention— this contact— is starting a fire between my thighs. Images of us together in my bed flooding in, the softness of his hair, the animalistic grunts he made. I squeeze my eyes shut tighter and let out a shaky breath, and refuse to accidentally glimpse the sight of some scaly, slimy, disgusting fish of any kind. The scent alone in the room makes my nose crinkle.

"Just a little further," Devin whispers in my ear— and my stomach flips over itself.

The air around us becomes cooler again and through my eyelids I can tell the room we just stepped into is carpeted and much brighter than the tunnels.

I still refuse to look until I hear Devin in my ear again, "Okay, open your eyes."

The second I open them, I am confronted with a sight cuter than I could have imagined. Little black fluff balls are gliding around on ice slides. Some stand and ruffle their feathers, while others dive into the clear blue water that surfaces at the glasses' middles in small waves.

They all seemed to be wide awake and fluttering around, until the lights dim slightly and a zoo keeper— wearing khakis and overly large rain boots— tugs into the enclosure with a bucket.

All the penguins giddily scurry towards her, the larger ones attempting to pop their heads into the bucket for an early meal.

"Oh it must be dinner time," I say, whipping my head to face Devin. He is smiling at me, not even having looked at the penguins yet. He nods slightly before a deep flush of red spreads across his cheeks once more, then faces the glass. We settle in close to the corner, watching the penguins catch tiny fish as the keeper throws them into their mouths. I grimace at the sight slightly, until I feel Devin's hands on my sides again. His fingers trace the hem of my shirt under my jacket, then he loops his finger in the loop of my belt. Before pulling me close to him and settling his chin on my shoulder.

Everything about the gesture is intimate, but nothing about it makes me want to pull away. I realize that I really like him. Especially touching me. I don't like anyone touching me.

I like how he smiles at everything, especially things that aren't funny, but even larger when things are. I like that he knows how to make me feel wanted, especially in the bedroom. Unfortunately all of those things don't matter as much as the topic looming over our heads. I haven't told Devin about the branding incident with SRB yet. Mostly because I still know very little about how it is going to affect the school overall. Also because I had only just met with Holden about it this morning.

Holden asked me not to mention it to many more people, that he would be handling it with the university and with the Sigma Rho Beta and Trent himself. He told me not to worry about the meeting with the presidents— so that is all I can think about at the moment. Even as the tiny penguins loop around the keeper, and Devin's hands wrap around my torso— cradling me from behind. My stomach drops. Am I lying to him? I'm getting distracted on our date— on my birthday of all days.

"Oh shit," I mumble, my face going hot, I hadn't told Devin it was my birthday today. I honestly would have forgotten myself if my mom hadn't called me to wish me a happy twenty-first year on this planet, and Frankie hadn't gotten me flowers. The flowers that were sitting in a nice vase on my counter— ones Deivn would most likely see.

"What's wrong?" Devin's warm breath dances along the back of my neck.

I laugh hollowly, "You're going to think it's funny actually," I say knowing he will laugh immediately when

I tell him he accidentally planned an amazing first date on my birthday of all days. "It's my birthday." I say turning to face him.

He doesn't laugh though, he actually looks like I have struck him. "It's your birthday?" he parrots.

"Yes, but it's no big deal. I don't need a cake or anything." I say reaching for his forearm with my frozen fingers.

"Wait, how old are you turning?" His tone sounds a bit accusatory.

I straighten my back instinctually. "Twenty One." I say, definitely.

"Oh" he looks at the penguin enclosure again. "That's an important birthday."

"Devin?" I step away from the surrounding strangers forming around us, as they try to gawk at the enclosure. We are in a darker area of the viewing room, but I can still see a line form between his brows. "It's not a big deal." I repeat.

"Who made you feel that way?"

"I don't know, no one. It's just I have never been a fan of birthdays, especially my own."

"Well we have to get you a drink or something." He says, turning to glance around us like a drink cart is magically going to appear.

"No we don't." I say gripping his wrist to refocus him.

The contact seems to ease him slightly, "I am not sure where you got the impression that your birthday doesn't matter." He says, and hands find my cheeks. They cool my warmed skin slightly, but it's his firm gaze of hazel eyes that steady me. "You're extremely special and anyone who doesn't see that is an utter fool."

"I have something else to tell you." I say, feeling my limbs shake, and my eyes well with tears.

"Are you okay?" Devin asks, his hands falling away from my face. He guides us— with his palm on my lower back— towards an enclave labeled emergency exit. Nearly missing the stampede of visitors leaving the exhibit, now that the penguins are all fed and plump.

"I've just," I say then start again. "It's just." My palms find my face, and I can feel Devin wrap his calloused fingers around my wrists, gently pulling them away before I begin again. "I have just had a terrible week, and it's only tuesday."

"Right." He nods, but does not interrupt me.

So I continue, "and I can't really explain in detail, but somethings happened with some of my sorority girls and some-" I pause, knowing that the ball is going to drop, and this very new and fragile relationship— if one could even call it that— is going to change in some capacity.

I take a moment to memorize Devins freckles and admire the tiny scar across the bridge of his nose that I haven't ever noticed. Everything about him seems so out of reach, yet he continues to stare at me, penetrating my soul. I close my eyes, inhale through my nose and pull back my tears. The scent of pine tar body wash and rock star sex appeal wrapping around me.

"Some Sigma Rho brothers." I wait for any spark of anger, any refusal or fight of what I am saying.

"Right." he says, straightening his spine, his hand grasping the side of his necklaces he scans the few strangers walking past throwing questioning glances our way.

My heart rate sputters alive, and my breaths come in heavy gasps.

"You knew?" I hear myself ask, but the ringing that starts in my ears makes me want to cry again. I shove out into the crowd, forcing myself to look at the shoes in front of me until I am led through the darkness of the exhibit. Where I slam my hands on the bar to push the doors open. Freezing cold air hits my skin, but the severity of the chill is nothing compared to my need to get the hell out of this zoo.

Of course Devin knew what had happened. "Fuck!" I shout into the air and the few snowflakes falling hit my face as I stand in the middle of the path. A few other visitors cast angry glares in my direction and tug their children away from me.

"Elle!" Devin shouts as he emerges from the exhibit behind me. I don't turn right away—instead I'm sucking a few breaths in through my nose and closing my eyes again— hoping my heart takes a hint and calms as well.

My name is called in the wind again and my anger buds alive despite trying to remain calm. "What?" I demand, turning to face him. He seems more upset than he was when I told him it was my birthday. Which for all I care, he should feel bad.

"I wasn't a part of it." He says, looking over my head. "Can we please sit down?"

He's doing that thing where he doesn't touch me all of the sudden, instead guiding us towards a bench with an open palm. Herding me like an angry sheep being chased by a collie.

"I know you were with me. I'm not stupid." I say crossing my arms over my chest, my puffy black jacket deflating slightly as I do. Despite being so angry with him, I sit down on the cold metal bench at the edge of the path, and frown. I force myself to look straight ahead at the light display of a kangaroo jumping up and down.

"I never said you were stupid." Devin says, gently sitting down next to me. Placing his elbows on his knees, but tilting his body towards me. "I just want to make sure you know I wasn't a part of it. That I don't agree with any of it. I only found out about it today. Trent was telling me that Holden called him into his office."

"You just found out about it today?"

"Yes, I was going to ask about it, but I didn't want to ruin our date."

"Our date?" I ask. Feeling silly that, with a single sentence, Devin has managed to melt my exterior frost.

"Yes," Devin grins wildly, before looping his fingers into my crossed arms, pulling on them gently. I release my hold with some resistance, so he loops our fingers together and I am grateful for the warmth of them as he rubs his thumb in a gentle motion along the back of my hand.

Devin wasn't one of the men who had branded my sisters, he was simply one of the mass of them that would be associated with this scandal. I was all too familiar with the fact that one person could drag the name of their chapter through the mud. I expected he would defend them. Argue for his brothers with every breath, but he hadn't. He managed to be more mature then I could imagine a fraternity man being in a situation of this gravity.

"Now," Devin says, scanning my features again, "Can we please go get you a drink?"

"I would really like to just get a bottle of wine and go back to my place." I say, standing. My legs are stiff from sitting on the icicle blanketed bench.

"Yes Your Highness, anything for you." Devin says, wrapping his arm around my shoulder, then placing a kiss to my temple, before leading us towards the zoo's exit.

Chapter Twenty-One

Tuesday

DEVIN

"**I** don't think I have ever had sex on my birthday." Elle says and I can't help the laugh that bubbles out of me. Her head is on my chest and in the faint light of her living room, I can't see her face but I can tell she is smiling. Solely from the movement of her cheeks on my stomach, but her body also shakes to match the sound.

We made it to the couch and drank half the bottle of wine before she knelt in front of me and took me in her mouth. I had every urge to let it finish there, but I knew it wasn't very gentlemanly to do so on her birthday, so after I pulled her onto my lap— as we undressed, and kissed, and felt each other in new ways— the rest of the movements fell into sync.

"This birthday is special, so you get whatever, Your Highness."

"Why do you call me that?" She asks, angling her gaze to meet mine, and her blue irises make the butterflies in my stomach lurch.

"You're a queen, and I want you to never forget that."

"I'm just the president of my sorority." She giggles, shuffling herself deeper into the space between my legs— pulling on the blanket draped over us so that it's tucked just below her chin.

"That's not what I am talking about." I say, watching her eyelids flutter closed. Her toes brush my calves and my jaw ticks. "You are the most amazing woman I have ever met, before you I felt like I was treading water. Now," I clear my throat of the lump that's forming, "Now I wake up and check if you have texted and when I see your name across the screen and the photo we took I can't help but smile. You are extremely intelligent, especially when it comes to how to handle other people. Every cog in your brain works in mysterious ways. Honestly I'm envious of you, you don't care what anyone thinks about you. A true queen amongst her people."

"But you're always smiling," she says, softly.

"I only genuinely smile when I see you. You are so unapologetically yourself."

"Says the man who has no issue dancing in his sneakers."

"My mom always danced." I say, allowing my eyes to fall closed, "It was my favorite thing about her. Even though she was depressed, she always danced with me when we made dinner."

"Tell me about her."

"My dad pretends she didn't exist," The anger that threatens to leave my skin buds, but I suppress it by dragging my fingers through Elle's hair. "And I guess I held her in my heart. Hiding her from the world, because I didn't want anyone to tell me she wasn't real."

"But she was real." She says, lifting her head to meet my eyes, and my head falls back to evade her gaze. My eyes sting as I attempt to close them off from spreading any emotion.

"I know. Her birthday was on April 22nd." I whisper, and delicate her finger tips dance over the number tattooed on my ribs.

"Can I ask how she died?"

I'm silent for a brief moment— I'm ready to say the word, but knowing that when I do everything cements itself further. My heart constricts like it always does when I am reminded that she is gone. Like every time I say it, "suicide."

"Devin," Her voice is thick, and even behind closed lids I can tell she is crying for me. She doesn't ever let sad tears fall— I witnessed it first hand, even an injury couldn't even pull them out of her, but now she's shedding them for me. I feel the moisture drip onto my skin and her empathy mixes with my pain in a way I am not familiar with, but open to accepting all the same. "I can't imagine," she whispers.

"It happened years ago, and I had to see a lot of professionals. I took medication for a while but I stopped after—." I pause, not ready to divulge more about myself than I already have. Wanting to go back to the cheery air we had moments ago. "Before I came here. Where I met you."

"Right," she says, lowering her head to my chest again. "I'm so glad I met you," she whispers and the heat from her breath calms my nerves.

"I'm glad I met you too, Elle." I say. I want to say more, I want to tell her that I want to see her everyday. That the moments we've had together make me feel important and empowered. That for the first time I've felt seen and heard. That I could fall madly and desperately in love with her— but I don't.

We have so much time, that I know when she says it first I'll be jumping at the chance to reciprocate it. But I have to talk about my past in order for her to truly trust me and the fear that she will not understand falls like a rock in the pond and I sink at the idea of losing even the small pieces I have of her.

She seems to be in a better mood, despite the recent dive into my past and the since we discussed the incident with our two chapters. I had known we would eventually have to discuss it, but I had hoped it wouldn't come up until after the impending social event on Thursday.

All of it is inevitable, but inside our little bubble it seems like nothing else matters. The scent of her vanilla shampoo and the sound of her laugh. Her witty commentary, and soft spot for fuzzy creatures and gas station bags of chips. The way she moans when she eats. The way she moans when she comes. All of the tiny pieces of her that I could never be replicated by anyone.

Jinny was going to love her too, everything about Elle made me believe they would be great friends. Jinny would need her company along with mine next year. Honestly, anyone was better than Trent and my brothers being around Jinny, but Elle would be a great influence for my little cousin.

Trent would handle all the issues with the Sigma Rho Beta brothers and he would apologize for the incident. He wasn't vicious— he was doing the best he could. I hope Elle can understand that as a fellow president. She had always been against the development of Trent's all Greek Space, and now this wasn't going to help. Something deep in me, probably Trent's voice inside my head, knows I can get through to her. Maybe Trent was right and being her friend— or more than friend I guess— will help her see that despite this last incident. Trents proposal could be mutually beneficial. Maybe even help them get over this hiccup.

"You know he's doing all of this for us." I say, brushing my palm over her dark brown hair. She doesn't move or say anything right away, so I am unsure if it landed. She may have fallen asleep, it has been that long since either of us last spoke.

"You mean Trent?" She says, sitting up and abruptly pulling up her shirt from its place on the floor.

"Yes?" I say, meaning for it to be a statement but the sound of my voice grows at the end so I sound like I'm asking a question unintentionally.

She releases a breath and slides her shirt back over her head.

"You don't have to get dressed." I say, smiling at her, but she doesn't look at me.

"Yes I do, Handsome." She huffs, then continues, "I am not discussing Trent while my tits are out."

At the mention of her tits, I realize I do indeed want them out, and am ready to argue when she says, "I'm not exactly sure what you mean."

"I mean, Trent, he's trying to get this space, you know," I say, swinging my legs around her so we are both seated facing the dark screen of her television. I can see the gaze as it races around the room, intentionally avoiding me. "This space for all of us, and I know this thing isn't going to help but—"

"Thing?" She demands, reaching to our feet and finding her pants in their crumbled pile.

Anger— I can see it plainly across her face. She's doing wonders holding it all in, but it's there. I clearly see it, being accustomed to how anger likes to express itself. I try to remain unmoving. Every fiber in my body wants to reach for her, but I want to be sure I don't respond immediately. I'll let her be heated, but I need to remain impassive.

"Devin, you realize my sisters were branded like cattle." Her voice shakes but it's louder than before.

I'm frozen, unsure what to say or do, so I look at my hands. This seems to frustrate her so she continues yelling and the crack in her voice burns my soul, "forever they will have to be scarred with a stupid mistake, all because those men harmed them."

"I know," I say, unsure what else I can even say to that argument. I don't know the brothers that have done this personally, but I also don't know the entire story. The entire fraternity is trying to handle it in an expedient manner. Trent hardly told me anything, just that it needed to be over with soon, so that when he had to speak on it in front of the school it was able to be expressed that we did indeed "handle it". Someone would have to get blamed, have to get punished, maybe even forced out. I knew the procedure all too well. The school would need to hear that it was over— that the sororities forgave them. They had to, but Elle's face shows so much hatred I am not sure how to back track. How can I?

"I don't know what to say."

"I think you should go, I have an early class tomorrow." She says, hands on her hips and eyes scanning the carpet. Avoiding looking at me.

"Fine," I hear myself say, everything else is a fog. I dress in a daze, aim for the door. She is behind me, leading me away from the oasis. I am so unsure where we stand or how to fix it.

"When can I see you next?" I turn to face her with my hand on the knob of the door.

"I have a really busy next few days, so," I turn to her, cupping her cheeks in my hands, and surprisingly she lets me. I kiss her, firm and deep. Grasping for her to let me be who I am when it's just the two of us. Then I kiss her forehead and her arms circle around my waist.

Stepping out this door means bursting the bubble—means facing what really stands between us. All the things that make it hard for us to be together. All while we just started *whatever* this is. All while I think I am standing here holding the women I think I can love, all while I doubt knowing what to say about any of this. Or if she even knows how to handle it alone, I have to leave her to it though. She has more than enough capability to make the best decision for her organization— and she likes being in Greek Life. I have to remind myself that she won't blame all of us for a few rotten apples. She can't. I want to say that but she's pulling away, and opening the door for me.

I am in the hall with a few last words and I say that I'll text her. She nods in response, then closes the door. Leaving me more confused than I was yesterday and deathly afraid that if I leave now, everything will be different.

I pull out my phone and quickly send a text off to Jinny, expecting her to be asleep by now.

i fucked up

Jinny: What happened?

i'll call you tomorrow

Jinny: Okay, well I am sure you can fix it.

Chapter Twenty-Two

Wednesday

ELLE

I'm the first one to the president's meeting, so I sit in the spot that has the clearest view of the door. I know Trent also prefers this spot, but I can't get over the small part of me that doesn't truly care about his feelings.

"Elle." He announces boisterously, in a form of greeting, I am startled into my seat, forced to reign in my composure.

I greet him back, but it sounds as half hearted as I meant it to come out. He texted me a few times since the incident was brought up to Holden but we haven't talked directly about it. It's inevitable, but I don't want to be the one to bring it up. He should apologize— that's what I have decided— and anything less will not be acceptable. He needs to make sure the girls are okay— that's what will win him points in my eyes. He is shuffling his papers around, avoiding my gaze, so I take the same approach.

As I reach down to set my tote bag on the floor and grab a pen from the inside pocket, I notice he is staring at me.

I let the bangs fall across my face to conceal me from the awkward moment.

He clears his throat but I make sure to drag my finger tip along the folders I have in my bag— pretending to be searching for something. It would look weird if I did not collect anything— so I wrap a firm grip around my phone, along with a pen, from the inside pocket.

I haven't looked at it in a few hours, and I realize I missed a call from my–. My heart skips, I stare at my screen expecting this to be a sick joke. My dad's caller ID is staring back at me. He called me an hour ago and left a voicemail. Bile rises in my esophagus. I hate this feeling, I want to avoid this feeling at all costs. I don't typically mind confrontation— I was just about to go a round worthy of time in a penalty box with Trent, but now I want to curl in a ball in the back of my closet and never come out.

Ideas circulate in my mind. What could he possibly want? Listening to his voicemail means I'll have to hear his voice. Which may or may not actually make me throw up, since it's been like a year since I heard it. Inevitably, it'll rattle all my emotions around like a bad deck of cards all spewing out of an improper bridge shuffle. I want to ignore it. But I also want to know what he has to say.

It's been since my birthday last year that he even bothered to call. It was the day before and he had still managed not to mention the fact that I was turning 20 or that I was in my second year of college. All he managed to ever talk about was himself— how he was planning to move to Florida. The words, "I have nothing left for me here, so I need to go" still burned into my memory, and kept me away from reaching out to him first.

I straighten my spine, my ears garble like I am underwater, and it isn't until I face Trent that I realize he's talking to me. His mouth flapping and his black eyebrows crease together. He shifts his gaze to my phone then back to my face.

"What?" I ask, slamming my phone on the table abruptly.

"Ah putain," Trent grumbles, "What's wrong?" He's staring at the palm that is covering my screen, like he will be able to read the message if he tries hard enough.

"Nothing," I breathe, "just some personal stuff."

"Alright." He says, wrinkling his nose, before pulling out his own phone and typing away rapidly.

I stare at him, and the urge to argue with him strikes me deep. He most likely will rip me apart, but at least we will be talking about it, instead of ignoring what is going on. We have a few minutes before someone walks into the room, maybe he'll show a different side of himself finally.

He is after all wearing a— wait is he wearing a tee shirt? And it's blank, a flat grey color, no SRB letters in sight.

"Actually—," I fold my palms together atop the table and tuck them under my chin, resting my elbow on it to steady how shaky I am feeling. I don't think this will go in a way that is productive, but I have to try. "I was wondering if you have anything to say to me."

He lifts his gaze from his phone and noting my posture, sets his phone face down on the table and crosses his arms. "I do, but I don't think we should discuss anything without hearing from Holden first."

"Why?" I huff, letting my arms fall away from under my chin, his dark eyes rake over me. I don't necessarily like how they stop near my chest. I am also wearing a t-shirt today, and mine dips into a low cut over my breasts— I was hesitant about wearing it for just this exact reason. The weather temperature on my phone app is of course oddly high right before the week of Thanksgiving— that's how Colorado likes to work. "Do we need a referee?"

He doesn't respond to this, picks up his phone again and flips his thumb over the screen.

He reads the message he finally finds aloud, "Trent Turner, Sigma Rho Beta HQ has reviewed your formal request for a retrial hearing for your members." He pauses, his eyes skimming over sentences that are obviously more confidential, until he says, "the request is denied, we ask that you please deactivate those members' statuses immediately."

"Can they make you do that?"

"Well it's like you always say, fraternities are run differently than sororities." He doesn't elaborate, or even have time too, because Holden strides in the door, followed by the rest of the five presidents. His lack of emotion for the subject does not elude me.

We exchange pleasantries with the rest of the group, and Holden begins reviewing the topics we are going to discuss.

"Pardon," Trent pipes up and my ears burn. I want to interrupt him for interrupting Holden. "Can we discuss the All Greek Space again?"

"Of course." Holden quips, nodding towards Trent— who then continues his prior line of thought.

Multiple heads turn in my direction as he speaks on recent events— being sure to leave out basically all of the details— and Alicia's smile is small enough for me to realize they all understand what's going to happen in today's meeting. That they all already know about the branding incident. I clench my hands in my lap, knowing my adrenaline is throbbing against my vein walls. The sensation is familiar to me, having stepped on the ice

during a impactful game or when I forgot a sisters name—
she'd come in late to formal meeting and I had no choice
but to ask her to tell me who the fuck she was because I was
still reeling over Dakota's mental break down over changes
in the executive board grade point average requirements
had been pushed up again by head quarters. Needless to
say the sister— the one who's name I will never forget
again— still tells the humorous tale to any person who will
listen.

This feeling feels worse than that, but all the same. One
you know only holds heavy weight in the moment but that
is like an elephant sitting on your chest. I am fixing to fight
and my body knows it. All the heavily fueled loyalty I feel
for my chapter bursting out of me with one fell swoop
when Trent stands.

"I think I have everyone on board already, but I was
hoping to answer any questions you may still have." Trent
gestures his hands in the air, his grin of flashy white teeth
doing little to hide his pretentious nature.

"I don't think our chapters should be rewarded for some
false allegiance and unity." I say, abruptly, I can feel my
tears at the back of my eyes forming, so I stop and swallow
the lump building in my throat. "We're all pretending that
we all get along. When in reality we harm one another
every other week. Gossiping and tearing each other down

with our words, then physically harming members the next day."

"I told you we handled the issue." He glares at me with his piercing brown eyes. "The *internal* issue. Surely that does something to help change you and your chapters mind"

"Nothing will change our mind." I say, and it takes everything in me not to say it through gritted teeth.

Trent doesn't falter at my words, he simply sits back down. A small smile tugging at his lips before Holden directs attention back to him.

I leave the room hastily, attempting to not talk to anyone, especially Trent. Not even Holden could say anything about the interaction helpful enough to soothe me.

My phone pings in my bag and I stop in the hall, hiding out of the way near a water fountain to fish it out.

Devin SRB: hey, how was the president's meeting?

Nothing significant! Did you go to class or no?

I replay the entire conversation with Trent and the meeting in my head all day. I hardly focus on the few classes I have and by the time I am sitting down in my chair around the giant oval table for the Executive Board meeting, I realize I didn't eat at all today. My stomach assaults further with pangs of hunger— to really send home the reminder.

"Do you have any changes?" Laura asks as she hurries in and starts placing squares of paper— containing the loosely followed Robert's Rules of conduct agendas— in front of each seat. "I just printed these based on our conversation."

I reach over my shoulder to intercept my copy from her as she passes behind my chair. My eyes scan over the Times New Roman font quickly— jumping down to the section that is labeled: Presidents, under the reports section.

<u>**Executive Board Meeting Agenda**</u>

Call to order
Roll Call
Reports
   Archon:
      Social on Thursday
   Vice Archon:
      Appointing Social Chair for Spring
   Bursar:
      Dues increase for next semester/ discuss budget issues
      for end of year Formal dance.
   Judicial:
      Reminder of hazing policy
   New Member and Sisterhood Development:
      Big Application Review
   Recruitment:
      Ideas for Spring Recruitment Theme
   Academic Excellence:
      Study group updates
   Panhellenic Delegate:
      Spring Recruitment updates
   Risk Management:
Old Business
      SBR Event Space Issue
         Updates & Vote.
      Election Council Updates
New Business
      Executive Board Elections/ New Interviews Protocol
      Leadership Conference (February 19th-21st)
      Spring Retreat

"I need to talk about the SRB Event Space thing." I say, before finishing reading.

"It's under Old Business." Laura says, sitting at the head of the table. "I am assuming we are taking a vote on it Sunday."

"Right," I confirm, "and no risk management report?"

"Frankie never sent me anything."

"Okay," I run my eyes over the paper again, "I'll talk to her."

"I already did."

"Perfect."

"Did you read through the constitution again?" Laura asks, adding a note to her own agenda, before clicking the pen and tilting her gaze up to meet mine.

"Yeah" I say solemnly, "and I have a copy in my bag in case we need it tonight."

"I can't believe Kelly dropped." Laura says, her deep brown eyes tracing my face.

"Yeah, me either," I'm not sure how to react to my little leaving the chapter. It took a matter of minutes on Sunday for the entire chapter to be gossiping about what happened. Then worse of it all, I was approached by other members asking for my opinion.

Much like the previous issue from today with my dad, I follow the same approach. Dissociation is always the first response, then nothing but numbness follows. I had to move on. I have too many things I can be focusing my attention on instead. There was nothing I could do, Kelly was one of the wildest members in our chapter, despite being the Archon's little. Even under the circumstances, the fact of the matter was— I had nothing to do with her judicial hearing, or with her punishment of not being able to attend the year end formal ball that the sorority held every year. I had no control or genuine connection to her— and we both knew that fact— so when she decided to file a formal request to "drop out" of the chapter in spite of her hearing's results I didn't hear from her, and I wasn't sure if she'd want to hear from me. I had briefly mentioned it to another one of my littles it but I didn't want to "gossip", so I stopped asking for further information.

Devin was all I could think about without it hurting my brain or my heart. The fact that I was now actually failing my college algebra course also loomed. So I forced the rest aside, thoroughly convincing myself that if it wasn't directly associated with me or keeping my chapter running that I didn't need to bother thinking about it.

I felt awful about our fight, he was unaware of how much it was weighing on me, especially when it came to his brotherhood. But even on my worst day, seeing his text pop up made me smile— especially knowing my responses also made him happy. He was the only person I had texted with today outside of Laura. I won't be able to see him until the social tomorrow, not with his mandated meeting with his executive council hosted by SRB's Vice President. He has far less Greek obligation than I do— but Wednesdays seem to be the most conflicting for the both of us.

We've already agreed to really have a discussion about everything after the social event this week. So I lean into the chaos of the executive board meeting and my full class schedule the next day, knowing that staying busy will make that time come much faster.

Chapter Twenty-Three

Thursday

DEVIN

Jinny: Finished my finals! Can I come earlier?

how much earlier i have a social event tonight but tomorrow i am free

Jinny: Don't you have 2 classes tomorrow?

yeah do you want to go to those? or we can see a movie or something

Jinny: You should really go to class, I'll text you when I am an hour out. Where's the social event? Just in case I come early, can I meet you there? And Elle?????

No. ok. Place is called spinning pins. And no.

Jinny: How are you one of the smartest people I know, yet you are terrible at forming sentences via text.

maybe i am dumb

Jinny: and maybe I am the reincarnation of the great Jane Austen.

you might be.

Jinny: STFU

Bowling alleys smell like dirty feet. There is no nice way to put it, and even though Spinning Pins is the nicest and largest bowling alley in Conifer Valley, it's also the oldest.

Balls thud against the wood of lanes and pins crash all around me as I stride up to the pale pink plastic counter. The man behind it has a can of odor repellent and a shoe tipped upside down as a foggy mist sprays into the air around him with a heavy hissing sound.

"Hey man! I have a few lanes reserved. Under Devin." I say, maintaining some distance— to not inhale the cans contents that are now floating around in the air.

"Lanes thirty-five through forty, mate. The chick already checked you in." Hard rubber shoe soles hit the counter after I give him my size and I grip them by the heel counter. He lazily extends his hand around the desk— pointing towards the back of the alley— Elle falls into view under the neon glow of the lights.

She's shuffling around the tiny plastic tables, carrying two neon green bowling balls that seem would weigh down a person of her size with great ease. Placing them in differing pinsetter stales, then glancing up at the television screens as she types in her name with the tiny stiff keypad.

Her beautiful brown hair is pulled into small braids leading to small puffs at the base of her neck. Her soft tan skin accented by the pine green shirt with bright pink KSI letters across her chest is finished with a casual pair of light blue flared bottom jeans that also manage to hug every inch of her perfect figure.

Another girl with shiny black hair, and light brown skin hurdles down the stairs right past me, heading towards Elle. She doesn't even stop to greet me, simply shuffles her bag higher on her shoulder— like Elle does when she's in a hurry. She immediately starts spouting information that makes Elle brows form a tight line in the middle.

I haven't seen her work directly with any members at this point, and this seems important, so I stop. Instead fiddling with the rack of bowling balls to my left and watch the pair of them discuss things and shuffle more items around. Elle calls over to one of the servers and he lingers next to her a bit longer than I like, causing me to force myself to shout her name. The sudden change in volume in the otherwise empty end of the bowling alley causes both her dark haired sister and her to look up from the phone they are glancing at.

"Perfect!" Elle lights up, when she sees me descending the stairs, her smile causing the girl to stare at her face with a crinkled nose before she gazes at me with scrutinizing brown eyes. "Laura, this is Devin." Laura and I exchange pleasantries but hers is more than reserved.

"We were just ordering some food and soft drinks from the waiter before everyone gets here." Elle's magnificent blue irises glance back at the menu on her phone screen briefly before extending it out to me. "Did you have any suggestions?"

"Mozzarella Sticks." I say, without removing my eyes from her face.

Elle looks towards the waiter and he repeats the long list of appetizers and sodas before adding mozzarella sticks on the end and then he disappears.

The music in the bowling alley is some old R&B hit from when I was a freshman in high school and I almost mention it to elevate the silence that has stretched but Elle interrupts my thoughts.

"Laura is my Vice President." She says, glancing around me towards the door. "Did you come alone?"

"Yeah, the rest of the guys are meeting me here." I refrain from telling her that I walked. I busy myself with the laces on my sneakers before slipping them off and replacing them with the bowling alleys required. I know it's not a long distance back to campus but for some reason I know she will fuss if I make that common knowledge and she already seems tightly wound.

"Are you okay?" I ask as a stand, unsure what can of worms I will open with that question.

"Yeah, of course!" She says in a tone I don't really recognize.

"Are we okay?" I ask, dipping my head down towards her, so Laura doesn't hear us.

"Yes," she says looking towards Laura— who is inconveniently moving close to us. I don't know how Elle wants me to act, or if we are even supposed to be acting. I want to be myself so I decide that's what I'll do. I drape my arm around her shoulder and she stiffens slightly before gripping around my torso briefly. The sensation that the gestures sends down my spine and through my toes is intoxicating. I don't want her to let go, but the side hug she is giving me is the least intimate we have ever been while touching so I let go and search the rack of balls in the pinsetter.

"Are you good at bowling?" I ask, turning back to see her standing with her arms across her chest. Laura has moved further away now, and I wonder if Elle has mentioned me to her or any of her sisters. The urge to ask her that blocks my mind until I force it down— reminding myself that we are remaining low key about everything. Especially tonight. She doesn't like my fraternity very much, and I am sure her sisters share the sentiment if Laura's reaction to my arrival is any indication.

"Is any one *good* at bowling?" She says, punctuating the word good with an air quotes gesture.

"They have competitions, you know." I say, picking up a ball etched with the number 14 on it. Before swiveling it between my two palms.

I move to step onto the track and out of the corner of my eye I see Elle step up to the pinsetter.

"I think you're supposed to put your fingers in the hole." I know she doesn't mean it as an innuendo but those words and her voice make my body twitch and I turn towards her, smirking before I twist the ball back around my torso and toss the ball down the middle of the track. It glides in a perfect spiral and knocks into the front pin— scattering the rest in its wake. A perfect spiral. Not my best, but it definitely looked impressive.

Or so I think until I turn towards Elle. Her eyebrows are contorted and her smile is covered by her palm, blatantly attempting to force her laugh to stay in her body but struggling doing so.

"What?" I ask, laughing at the sight of her wild expression. "Did I look funny?"

"I don't think being good at bowling is as hot as you think it is." She says, her laugh escaping her at the end of the jab.

"That wasn't even a good throw." I say, and she laughs harder. Drawing Laura's attention to us again from the stall to the left.

The waiter comes and she finally quiets enough to thank him. He places four large pitchers of bubbling liquid on the table in our stall then hops over to the one Laura occupies— adding a few pitchers to her table.

I look up instinctually at the screen above me as I walk backwards towards Elle. Noticing that the name next to the X on the screen says, ED.

"Ed?" I ask her, finding her smile has faded from her previous amusement.

"I thought we could bowl on the same turn," she flutters her lashes and I want to so desperately kiss her for labeling us as a collective, even if it is in a way we will only understand.

"Okay." I say, glancing down at her mouth as she drags her tongue across her bottom lip. That fucking tongue.

"AYYYYYEEEE!!" Shouts a voice that I instantly recognize as RJ. He leads a pack of my brothers into the pit of alleys, heading straight for me and pulling me into a tight embrace, before patting my shoulder hard as he normally does. Brooks and Geoff flank at his sides and I hold up a fist for them to pound. Both of them seem to be in a good mood, but no one is as loud about the fun as RJ.

I immediately know he has had a couple beers already, his navy blue tee shirt smells like shitty PBR. Elle shuffles away, and I can't help but question if I should have told them not to drink before this event.

I try to compensate for my oversight by reminding each of them that it is a sober event— even though they are of age— so they need to wait until after the event before going to the bar. Geoff is the only one who seems to be genuinely taking in the information while the other two have found their way towards Laura. Who seems like she might punch them in the throat if they get too close to her.

I don't have time to speak to Elle again because more Greek members have arrived. Swarms of sorority sisters in matching outfits and hoards of brothers clambering to the appetizers as soon as they land on the little tables.

Trent shuffles in, phone in hand, wearing his black SBR polo and perfect shoes. Which I notice he doesn't exchange for the proper foot attire for the event. He seems to enjoy the brief conversation he has with Elle— but her body language is cold. A small part of me loves that, but I also hoped seeing them in public wouldn't cement that she hates our frat so deeply.

Hours fly by and I catch glimpses of Elle through the crowd and she bowls a couple rounds under our name and I let our score dwindle in the low seventies until she disappears in the restroom with a red head I think is her friend Frankie.

My phone buzzes in my pocket, but when I look for Elle she is still making her way to the bathrooms, so I know it's not important.

"Who's ED?" Brooks calls from the booth and I jump at the chance to toss the ball down the lane. Elle wasn't impressed but I know the guys will be. They hoot and holler for me when I get the last few X's on the board then throw for the extra strike, which barely pulls our score up to an over one hundred.

Elle and Frankie are perched above the pit at one of the high top tables and Frankie is talking exaggeratedly with her hands, but Elle sits perfectly still— seemingly enamored by her friend's tale.

I don't realize I am staring until Frankie meets my gaze and her hands fall to her side. Her red lipped smile widens and she turns towards Elle, who is finally looking my way before shifting her eyes quickly towards the back of the glowing bowling alley. I take the hint and vault the stairs, strutting past them without a second glance.

Shadows close around me and I hear the shouts from the fraternity men becoming muffled the further I step towards the emergency exit.

Arms wrap around me from behind, and I immediately know the hands crossed around my front are Elle's. I turn to face her and she lifts on her toes to peck a small kiss on my lips. I am stunned she wants to do this here but I am not going to complain. I lean down, gripping her jaw with my palm— pulling her face up to meet my kiss. She dances her tongue along my lips and I stroke it with mine briefly before parting them for her.

"Hi," she breathes, baby blue irises jumping up to meet my gaze then falling to my lips again.

"Hi." I say, bending and wrapping my palms around her thighs and hosting her up, before turning us to press her back into the thematic printed wall-papered wall. I kiss her harder this time, every once of my control slipping. I don't care if anyone sees, but I know she does. I can't help taking as much of *us* as I can before someone notices she is missing from the group.

Her legs wrap around my waist and I grind into her. My erection forms immediately. She moans, indicating I am not being subtle. We're a frenzy of heat and want— our lips only parting to adjust our heads. I kiss her neck, inhale the vanilla scent of her shampoo and my fingers tightens on her ass.

"What color underwear are you wearing?" I ask when I finally break for air. Before kissing her collarbone, noting the black straps of her bra, imagining they match.

"Purple," she whispers and I moan into her skin at the thought.

"My favorite."

"You said that about my black pair." She giggles, as I kiss her neck again.

"Well, those are now my second favorite." I say, stamping her harder into the wall so I can trace the hem of her jeans with my thumbs. Pressing into the ridge of her hips.

She laughs and I encompass the sound with my mouth on hers again.

"I said I'm fine!" A shrill voice announces at the end of the hall and Elle and I fly apart. Her feet hitting the floor as I turn to hide my bulge from the two people who have entered the hallway. My hands firmly land on the wall and I try not to act on my anxiety of being caught with Elle as it rattles around under my skin.

The couple hasn't noticed us yet but they are blocking our escape. The blonde hair girl firmly pushes against the solid form of the classic blonde crew cut haired man in front of her. He doesn't even budge, mostly because he is the size of Dwayne Johnson in his prime years but also because he seems to have his haunches on guard. His ink decorated tan skin bulges under his tight black tee shirt, but he doesn't shift his stance, even when the girl presses into his chest a few more times repeatedly.

"I told you to stay away from this. That I could handle it." The man's shoulder sag slightly and he catches her wrists as she folds her head into her hands, resting against his ink covered grip.

Elle springs into action before anyone else. "Hillary? What's wrong?"

Hillary immediately becomes alert and yanks her hands from the man's grasp, he doesn't move, just finds me with his eyes— blue like Elle's but even more striking. Somehow, all I can think about is how impressive his facial hair is, a decent length and very clean cut like his hair. If he is concerned about what just transpired between Elle and I it doesn't show, his gaze finds the side of Hillary's head as she turns toward us.

"Oh Elle," She gasps wiping at the tears falling over her cheeks. The man's tattooed hand falls to her lower back but she doesn't flinch, so I take it as a moment to relax slightly. "Yeah, we're fine. Just talking."

"Are you sure, do you want me to get Frankie?" Elle asks reaching to comfort Hillary, but the girls seem to be at an impasse. They both are apprehensive as their eyes dart amongst the four of us.

"No it's okay." Hillary finally says, her voice firm and her head tilted higher. "This is Max. He's in AEE. Just transferred in" Alpha Epsilon Epsilon is our buddy fraternity, but I don't recognize him.

Max jaw twitches at the statement and his eyes bore deeper into the side of Hillary's head.

"Devin." I reach my hand out— mostly as a distraction—and he reciprocates with a firm tug, and an even firmer smile. "I am a transfer too."

"Nice to meet you." Max says, his voice is calm like the rest of him, despite his obvious discomfort. He doesn't seem to be a threat to Hillary at all— they are obviously just a couple in a heated conversation.

We all step out of the mouth of the hall and back into the neon-lit bowling alley, the sounds of balls crashing and fraternity men bellowing picking up again.

I look up to find Trent headed for us and I take a step towards him, hoping he doesn't see how close Elle and I are to one another. I know she isn't ready to make us public, and this is definitely not the time I want to do so either.

Panic starts to build in my gut. What if he already knows, and that's why he's headed over here. The thought is shattered by the sight of the dark blond haired pistol that flies around him and my smile jumps up to a full blown grin at the sight of her.

"J?"

She barrels past Trent at a run, her tiny long black cardigan flowing around her fishnet tights. Only Jinny would wear denim shorts and flimsy tights in winter and call it *fashion*. Maybe it was, who am I to judge? I don't even know where my jacket is.

"I texted you," she shouts, before jumping into my arms for a quick hug, her large black leather bag flying and hitting my side as she does.

I twirl to find Elle, staring at the both of us and I mouth an apology which she accepts with a simple smile. Hillary, Max, and her awkwardly shifting their gazes between the three of us.

Trent grimaces at the sight of all of us, but he joins the small huddle.

"You must be Elle." Jinny announces looking right at her. They match up in height but Jinny looks so much younger as she leans across the space to hug Elle. "You're so much prettier than Devin described."

"And this is Hillary and Max." I say introducing everyone I can that remains in the vicinity. All gazes shift to me and I clasp my hands together in the midst of the awkwardness. "Well." I announce, "Jinny you shouldn't be here."

"What!" she demands, "why?"

"Because you're underage and this event is for college students only." I look around hoping not to catch any of my brothers goggling at the girl who is more of a sister to me than a cousin.

"I am going to be in that demographic in a few months." She whines before shuffling towards the crowd of SRB brothers who pass us on their way to the bar. I look at my watch, noting how they waited exactly one minute after the social ended to get intoxicated.

"No." Trent and I state in sync, as Jinny turns towards him.

"I. Hate. You." Jinny spits, and to my suprise, her gaze is firmly on Trent when she punctuates the words.

"I'm taking you back to my dorm." I say, splaying my palm out to herd her back towards the front of the bowling alley.

"I can take her," Trent says and Jinny's nose crinkles in disgust. "You should finish clearing up the event. Since you're the chair."

Hillary and Max take that as an excuse to leave our group, and Hillary scoops up her bag from one of the booths before swiftly heading for the exit— Max quickly on her heels, pleading for her to slow down.

Despite Jinny's lack of enthusiasm for Trent, the two of them have known about each other for years.

"Okay," I say, my eyes falling on Elle. She's biting her lip, and the sight makes me pause briefly. "You're right, I should help Elle clear everyone out."

Trent grumbles something when they are a few steps out of ear shot and Jinny tosses her hair and a harsh "ah, ta gueule" at him, before stomping towards the exit. I feel slightly bad for him until I see the odd smile he flashes me before picking up his pace to open the door for her.

"Elle?" I ask coming up next to her as she tries to clean up the tables around the lanes that now lay vacant.

"Want to grab a drink?"

"Don't you have to go?"

"I can hang out for a little bit," I say, glancing towards the bar, "Jinny will be fine."

"With Trent?"

"Yeah now that you mention it, I am a bit worried about him." I say grinning at her, as she collects her tote bag from the booth and we walk over to the bar.

"Okay," Elle says, her lashes fluttering as she looks up at me, "but I have to study, so I can't stay late."

"One drink," I promise.

Elle's red head friend, Frankie, greets us as we enter the space that makes up the bar section of the alley. Then I am instantly comforted by Elle tucking into the booth on my left as we settle in and listen to the story RJ is telling the table— the one about the time he threw a eighty yard touchdown pass at his high school's homecoming game.

"It was probably more like fifty, but okay." Elles jokes and all heads turn her way, including mine. She smiles shyly, before she laughs. I can't help but laugh as well, then Frankie joins in and before I know it we are all joking with RJ. Swapping stories of the great plays we have witnessed in the respective sports we have all played.

I force away the growing bit of envy and hurt that I start to feel, as I swallow another gulp of beer. Before I lean back in the booth to watch Elle completely blossom with other people like I have only seen when we are alone. A regal queen amongst her people, relaxed and having dare I say...fun.

Chapter Twenty-Four

Sunday

ELLE

My dad's getting married. That's why he called on Wednesday, to tell me that. Well and to inform me that he is no longer moving.

I've only listened to the voicemail once but his voice still haunts me, like always. I should be focused on the test I have first thing in the morning for my Leadership Issues class. Instead the sound of his voice followed me— circulating in my through my train of thought as I met with Leah and Laura before the Judicial board again. I was constantly reminded that despite being bombarded by my unresolved trauma that I do indeed have a chapter to run. Reminded the chapter was shuffling with angst— mostly the opinions about the recent events surrounding Kelly's departure. Sisters either blamed me for Kelly leaving— frustrated with me for not begging her to stay or digging my hands into the judicial boards business. Delusional to the fact that I had little power in the matter, despite my title.

Needless to say, as I stared out at the empty rows of chairs that formed the meeting room. While my executive board shuffled around me— dressing tables and whispering to themselves— I feel a deep urge to flee.

Knowing even that isn't an option. Even though the idea is very appealing. I have to power through, pretend nothing is wrong. Get over the fact that I want to be anywhere but in this room right now. It's times like these ones, where I know if I step out into the hall for a breath of fresh air that I won't find it. Instead all heads will turn to face me, watch me as a walk, all while hoping that I trip or stumble. Scrutinizing me for my actions or how I did my hair this week. If not their loathing, then they will idolize the false actions of a leader. Naive to the fact that I am— more often than not— simply someone being led by the puppet strings. They all expect some regal behavior surrounded by her council of members leading a charge, when in reality all I feel is completely and utterly *alone*. Even though I am surrounded by dozens of people, all of which I am supposed to call sisters, none of them seem to be as such. The few of us adorned with the title of presidency are warned that it isn't for the faint of heart, but damn they really did underplay it.

"Elle?" Frankie's voice breaks through my haze as she sits in the chair directly next to me. It's not her designated place in the line up, so she doesn't remove her bag from her shoulder or have on her black robe. "Are you okay?"

"Yeah, I just haven't eaten today, that's all." I flatten the table cloth in front of me, before adjusting the gavel to lay how I like it—resting slight askew on the sound block. It's auburn wood is smooth and tempting me to use it. I clutch my agenda in my hands instead— to resist the urge.

"Well, here." Frankie digs into her bag and pulls out a bag of cheesy crackers. "Eat some of these."

"No I couldn't," I say, shaking my head and trying to fixate my blurry vision on the paper in my hand.

"Well you can, and if you want to make it through this meeting you're going to have to. We're voting tonight right. It might be a long one."

"Right." I say shoveling a handful of the orange squares into my mouth.

Meeting is unremitting but swift, and votes happen without falter when following the sororities rituals or Roberts Rule of Order.

"All in favor for the all greek space headed by SRB say I"

Silence.

"All those opposed say I."

The "I's" are unanimous.

I leave the meeting first as ritual states and a slump against the wall briefly— I only have a few minutes of peace— but not much after that. The silent hall beckons to be filled with sisters and I will be forced to pretend that I am not affected, that I am willing to speak to them. That Kelly won't come up.

I say my farewells to the few sisters— half scowl at me, but some smile. All are rushing out of the meeting almost immediately, and I am slipping back into the room through the swarms. Nodding to each of them and masking it all with a smile. I hear faint whispers of biased opinions and my lack of compassion. "She was her big, you'd think she'd care," hits my ears and then from another sister, "Kelly was reckless". Many of them repeat the gossip: "She wouldn't be able to attend the formal dance anyways."

I will be able to go home soon, when the rest of the executive board leaves, and we are all cleared out of the room.

Frankie is at my side before I can flinch, helping me strip off my robe and handing it to Laura, as she collects them all and places them in the garment bag she is instructed to carry with her.

"Are you feeling better?"

"Yes, thank you." I say hoping she doesn't ask again— because I am not okay— but forming a coherent sentence that captures how I exactly feel seems impossible.

I rush to the collection of belongings that we hide in the small area considered the emergency exit. Itching to see if a certain person has texted me. I need to sleep tonight but a huge part of me wants Devin's arms around me as we hide from the world. His presence brings a sense of calm I have never felt before with anyone else and I'm over the fear of admittance.

My phone is blank when I get to it, but I know he is also in a meeting, so I send him a quick text. Hoping he is able to open it soon. That he'll respond quickly, and accept my offer.

Come over. Stay the night?

The rational part of my brain says all of this is crazy, but the other part tells me that I don't care. I want Devin and I am starting to wonder why I don't want people to know that. It'll change things, I will be forced to accept SRB for who they are. Even though my chapter— with my full support— just voted against their stupid idea to create and monopolize space on campus.

"The social was *great*." Says a sister as she passes me, and the compliment falls off me like broken glass to the floor. One of my other littles looks my way but quickly departs with her friends.

Hillary is at the table speaking to another sister— Ryann I think is her name. When I approach, she doesn't stop her discussion but throws me a sympathetic smile.

"Definitely apply for the position, you never know how the interview will go, it all depends on what the election council decides." Hillary says gently, placing her hand on the girl's arm before she scurries away.

"Ryann wants to run for Panhellenic Delegate next year." Hillary says to me, once Ryann is out of earshot.

"You aren't rerunning?" I ask, knowing Hillary is very good at her job.

"No," she says, collecting items before looking up at me. "I am running for Panhelenic President next year." I forgot we had the rotating seat this upcoming year.

Elections occurred in the Spring, but applying for them was expected at the beginning of the term. All the applicants will need to be vetted by the Election Council— interviewed, assessed in their current positions, even asked to attend a few meetings with the previous chair holder to deem their abilities and time commitments. I was the only one being considered for Archon, and a small part of me wondered when I had made that decision or if it was thrust upon me through assumption.

"Of course!" I say smiling widely, "you are perfect for it."

"Thank you, Elle." She says, shoving her arms through her long grey trench coat, "that means a lot coming from you."

"Really?" I say, before I can hold back the words.

"Yeah, you're a great Archon, I can only hope I can be as good as you."

I know she means the words. Hillary is too nice to not mean them. She is also very smart and more than capable of being a great president. I'm not sure why everyone seems to think it's some devine selection—that I didn't just decide to be in charge one day, despite all my lack of qualifications.

"You will be too." I say. I never quite knew what I was asking for when I became president. I thought I was in the stair stepper to power— the greatest position— but now, I am not sure if I agree with all that. But telling her — with her glowing eyes and so much hope— seems petty, so I say nothing more.

Instead I collect my items, hauling my tote bag's strap up onto my shoulder, and then head to my car. The air outside is cold, but holds a small torch to the winters in Minnesota, so I don't even bristle as I walk.

"Elle!" The voice that breaks the wind is so familiar that my knees buckle.

"Hey Handsome." I say before turning to see Devin, who is so nicely dressed I could swoon. He is dressed in black pressed slack pants and navy collared button up shirt, his black tie has been tugged loose, but his blonde hair is slicked back in a swoosh. This is a side of him that I am not used to— a side that I sort of like.

"You look great," I say on instinct.

"I was gonna say the same thing about you, Your Highness." He smiles and if it wasn't freezing outside my skin would be lit on fire.

"I texted you." I say.

"I responded," he says, closing the distance between us.

"Oh," is all I manage to get out before he's kissing me with cool hands at the base of my neck, before dragging up and through my loose hair.

A few hollers from fraternity men happen round us and he parts from our embrace, not even hesitating as he swoops and arm around my shoulder and leads me to my car— where he opens the driver door for me, then crosses over and hops in the passenger seat.

"So you want me to spend the night."

"Yes Devin." I say, turning the key and the heat kicks on, "I want you to stay the night."

He grins at me, and I can't help but smile back. There's just something about this overzealous man that is so damn *happy*, and being happy sounds perfect to me right about now.

Chapter Twenty-Five

Wednesday

ELLE

Devin hasn't responded to my texts since last night. He spent the night at his place for the first time in days. I finally texted my mom to mention him, and she even stopped her yoga to talk to me about him on the phone for over an hour last night.

I slept like shit when he left, but I had to refrain from begging him to come back because I am not too naive to realize that only two weeks have passed since I met him. I like where we are, where we seem to be headed, and the possibility of eventually announcing that we may be a thing.

He is insistent that we are exclusive, and that he wants this for more than our secret hideouts, quiet dates, and late night trips to the gas station. Getting used to his need for quality time and physical touch has been a hurdle— more on the first point than the second— but still his confidence in himself, in me, and in *us* is infectious. The way he looks at me is addictive.

I'm smiling widely at the photo of us when I realize that I am four minutes late to the president's meeting.

"Fuck," I mutter, scooping up my laptop and shoving it into my bag. Which I also realize is slightly lighter than usual because I forgot two of my binders. What was I thinking? Now I will have to relay the reasoning my chapter had of our votes based on memory alone.

The door to the small meeting room is closed but the windows expose the table, all attention seems to be on a presenter— who's hidden out of sight behind the wooden door— and I have a deep feeling Trent has already begun his third attempt at expressing his enthusiasm about the "All Greek Space".

I am already late. So there's no getting past the awkwardness that comes next, but I hate seeming out of breath and anxious in front of anyone so I attempt to slow my breaths and my strides. I'm now sweating under my green crew neck and the hair on the base of my neck sticks to my skin in an uncomfortable way. My hand is on the cool metal handle and I can hear Holden asking a question but don't hesitate to wait before turning it with a click.

"Sorry I am late–" I start to say, squeezing into the small space. The door falling closed behind me as I shuffle around space to the vacant chair next to Alicia.

My heart lurches into my mouth at the sight of Trent in his navy polo and tan slacks, cross legged and facing the television screen like the rest of the council. His smile is viscous, as he says, "No worries, we were just listening to an avocation on the 'All Greek Space' and why we should all vote yes on it."

My eyes flick to the front of the room. I am more than aware that my face gives away every once of my disappointment, because for the first time since I met the golden retriever of a man standing at the front of the room— wrapped in all his rock band tee and dark jeans exterior— he look's so *ashamed*.

"Elle–" Devin starts, but I shake my head.

"Please continue." I say, my gravel voice betraying me and the look Alicia flashes my way forces my tears to remain deep inside me, but the burn in my throat is straining as I do.

My ears pound and I don't hear a word he says, simply watch his dimple appear and vanish as he speaks. He points at the screen, but I don't look away from his mouth. The same mouth that worshipped my skin for less than a fortnight.

Suddenly I feel so young, fragile, and betrayed. I don't even care about the stupid "All Greek Space" anymore. I know that my vote won't change— I can't change it— my chapter has already decided its fate.

I let him into my bed, under my thick skin protecting my heart. Every situation seems tinted a sour grey instead of their previous rose. Trent knew about it all, he wouldn't be smiling if he didn't. They are friends, and have been since pre collegiate, I was stupid to have thrown that information aside.

Secrets were kept, on my end as well, but his are far more deceiving. A ploy from the beginning, to get me to go along with their game.

"He's doing this for us," are the only words that replay in my mind, Devin had said them loud and clear, I had just ignored them. Ignored the red flags in light of the dimples and compliments.

Now Trent thinks he can force my hand, that because I am facing Devin's plea that I won't vote no. Now, my walls climb back up, and brick by tedious brick I'll guard my heart. Now I can't be with Devin in any capacity, because I don't know if it was ever real.

"What sort of budgets will be required to help create and maintain this space." Alicia's question washes over me and pulls me back into the tide of reality.

"We will be requesting an allocation from the University, since we contribute to the largest campus extracurricular activity population." Trent responds and I have to give it to him. He's prepared and has played the long game well.

"And if they refuse?" I rebuttal, my gaze locked on Devin. He drops his gaze to his sneakers and his shoulders rise with a heavy breath. Good— I hope his heart rate is as high as mine.

"Well it's all a part of the proposal, so we will have to negotiate if it comes to that." Trent says dismissively.

A long moment stretches, then Holden further explains, "what Trent means is we will have to see if they are willing to discuss the plan as it is written or we will come back to the drawing board and re-frame the proposal."

"I understood." I give Holden a quick nod and return my stern look back to Devin. He is now forcing himself into the chair next to Trent and I can't help but furrow my brows.

"So can we vote now." Asks Trent, and my teeth grind.

"I don't feel comfortable allowing SRB to head this project with the recent situation that occurred with my chapter. My members agree that it wasn't handled as seriously as it was supposed to, by their chapter or the University." I say, each word quick and clipped.

"Those members were kicked out," Trent seethes, "that's not enough of a punishment?" He unfolds his legs from one another and leans forward until his elbows meet the table. The other five presidents remain so statuesque it's unnerving.

My anger shakes my spine, and I pray no one can see me tremble. I am confident in my decision and my ability to stand up for my sisters, but anger is expressed differently in everyone and unfortunately for me I sometimes cry when I get to my breaking point. I can't cry, even though Devins presence makes it so damn hard.

I swallow the lump in my throat hard and my voice cracks, "we were never apologized to, or even considered. We never fully discussed it." I glance around to the other presidents. All of them seem less than eager to speak up. All avoiding my eye contact, but all have their attention on the feud Trent and I are finally letting come to the surface.

"You want us to apologize." Trent expresses with little to no emotion painted on his face. "Then, we apologize."

I scoff, and Trent's jaw tightens. He has a mask that he wants to remain in place, and I realize at this very moment I could care less about what the fate of this "space" is. Trent can win, because I'm exhausted. Worn down, I guess, completely unsure why I cared so much in the first place. I can't control what others do, I can only control my own actions.

Realistically his apology should be enough, but I am flustered and words mean little to me at the moment. This meeting is ridiculous, I am a lone vessel in frigid waters. Nothing I say will change anyone's decisions. My chapter's decision— along with the other organization's choices— are already sealed.

"I'm ready to vote." I say, slumping back into my chair.

Holden conducts the vote and all but myself and Devin— because he has no privileges in this council to do so— vote yes. My sole aching voice is the only "I" when Holden requests to hear the opposed votes.

A laugh escapes me and my hands shake as I grip my belongings and flee from the room, tears cascading down my face as I do. The dam has broken and I can't hold them in any longer. Not only do I feel deflated and disappointed but completely defeated. I'm angry at Devin, but mostly at myself. For believing him, for falling for him, for contemplating loving him.

"Elle!" Devins voice trails after me, but I can't stop. I won't have this conversation here— in this space that was mine first. Now it's too messy for me to want to stay. I can't avoid him, I knew he'd hurry after me. Always consistent— hurting me then hurtling forward to make sure to try to fix me.

Cold air beats against my cheeks, as the doors are being held open for students as I pass. There are so many people around, so many witnesses to my pain. I pick up my pace, throwing myself towards the hill that leads towards the dorms. Unsure where I intend to go, just that I need to flee. I start to run but my tote bag weighs me down, so I stop at the first empty bench I see. Finally allowing myself to crumple with my head in my hands.

I know that I have a few moments before my peace bubble pops. My breaths are heavy and full of gusto as I try to slow my tears. I face my head to the sky, embracing the cold that the streak of moisture has left leading down to my upper lip and over the apples of my cheeks. Allowing my body to be drawn to a main point of the moment that I can cling to, the chill of the air, the cold metal through my jeans. The few flakes of snow that brush across my nose.

"Elle." Devins voice is small, and when I finally open my eyelids to see him, he is crinkled tight. His hands in his front pockets to protect from the cold, his bare forearms pebbled with bumps in the chill. His brows are forced together and the line between them resembles the previous dip of his dimples, now hidden as he frowns.

"None of it was real." I say, facing the sky again and letting my eyelids fall closed, briefly.

"Don't say that," Devin rushes forward, his arm flailing wide. I back away from him, leaning in my seat. "I'm sorry, can I please sit?"

I nod, my chin jutting out as I do. The line in the pavement suddenly is more interesting to look at than him. I feel him sit on the bench, he doesn't say anything but the breath he exudes is full of intention. I replicate the breath for myself, feeling my shoulders heave as I do.

"Why?" I ask and I hate that my voice is hollow.

"I–" he starts then stops, palming his face in his hands. From this angle he looks so different than I have seen him before. Every side I've seen now and I hate that a small part of me wants to comfort him in his discomfort. Like hugging will make the last hour dissipate and the things he's done run down the drain.

"I fucked up at U of C," he says into his palms, I hardly hear the entire thing, but I am hoping he continues before my anger bursts. "I was a midfielder on the varsity D1 team, my dream. But one night, at a party." He removes his face from his palms and faces me, his eyes swollen. He's raw, like no man I have ever seen— broken and not over what just happened but from something unrelated to us, but I can't excuse what just happened.

Hurt people, hurt people.

I'm not sure where I heard it first, but this is an example of that and he's attempting to rectify it, so I remain silent.

"The entire team was there, and a girl was found in the bathroom." He stops, pulling a palm over his lips like if he catches the words they will present less real. "I found a girl in the bathroom, she wasn't breathing."

"What happened?"

"She snorted something that was laced, I think, at least that's what the counselor said later. But I think she mixed some things, because I snorted some too, before I noticed her. The entire team was going to face a season cancellation, so I—"

"Devin–,"

"That's why I am here, they asked me to take the fall and I did. I was the one who found her so I could explain that I was the one who gave her the drugs. They temporarily suspended me from the team the next day." He stands and begins pacing the sidewalk in front of me.

"Who asked you?" I say, unsure if I know what to say exactly, he obviously has been dealing heavily with this for some time, but I can't excuse the events that have occurred just on these grounds alone.

"I was asked by my team captain. He said that I would be able to come back after the season. But he didn't know my dad would pull me out for good. That he'd be ashamed that I took the fall, even if it was an easy cop out."

"You told your dad you lied?" I clarify, my heart constricting for Devin all over again.

"Yes, he didn't care, said I wasn't going back there and that I needed to start fresh so I picked Conifer Valley. He still beat the shit out of me though."

"What?" Tears fill my vision again, but Devin doesn't continue, clearly unable to finish the conversation. "That wasn't your fault, her death didn't happen because of anything you did or didn't do. Your dad shouldn't let you feel like you needed to hide from that. He shouldn't—" Devin bristles in the wind and at the fact that we are finally discussing something so raw and real. I calm my nerves with a deep breath and finish. "You are so unbelievably kind, did you know that? Regardless of what has happened today or last semester, and despite your family's issues, you are a kind man. I have a feeling your mother would be proud of that fact. Though you haven't said much about her. I think she would be."

He nods but doesn't speak. Every once of my skin is pulling me to cradle him in an embrace, but that will remove my feelings from this situation and I can't do that.

He stops to face me, falling to his knees in front of me. The gesture is odd— but so on brand for him— and I am glad the classes for the hour have begun, because I couldn't handle anyone seeing him like this. "Elle, I am so sor—"

"Please—" I breathe, tears falling on my wrists, "stop." I tug at his elbows for him to stand, and he falls into the seat next to me. His knees brushing the side of my legs as he leans in to grab my hands. I clasp them firm, attempting to seem comforting, but completely unsure how I am still not ready to be touched. He needs this, so I do it for him. "Just explain. Please I am owed at least that."

"Trent asked me to be in the committee to help form the proposal, I didn't know that I didn't agree to the tactics of convincing you then, but it was after we met so—" he pauses and I can't help but try to decipher every word he might say based on his hazel eyes shifting across the back of my hand. "I didn't know how to tell you."

"Our first date?" I whisper.

He doesn't respond so I rephrase, "Were you on this *committee* the day you made me dinner? The day we—"

"Yes."

My heart hammers in my chest and the tears constrict in my heart again, this time I let them burst through. More drops fall down my cheeks but I don't dare to move otherwise.

"It was after the night at Silver Spur, but I didn't want to lie to you."

"But you did." I pull my hands from his.

"I didn't." His hazel eyes fixate on my face.

"Omission is the same as lying." I turn to him, forcing him to see the hurt in my expression. "Believe me you'd hate to hear that I lied about my feelings for you."

He rears back like I hit him, "I never lied about that."

"You know why I couldn't vote yes, why I hate your brotherhood," my voice rises and I hate the person I am becoming— since he made me feel so small, but she's already here. "I told you they harmed my sisters and you stood behind them to create a *facade* of unity."

"I didn't think—"

"I know. But you and Trent pressured me, hoping I'd say yes."

"That's not true–," he argues.

"Don't" I grit my teeth, "Don't tell me no, I'm not stupid Devin."

"I never said you were, Elle." He softens slightly but he isn't reaching for me anymore, and I can't help but retreat into myself more too. Remaining silent, because I'm not sure how much energy I have left for this man.

He rolls his lips together and moves to stand. "That's it then?"

"What?" I look over at him, confused about what else he could be so lost about. "You and Trent got what you wanted. To humiliate me, and win over the council. Congratulations." I lash out, consumed again by my anger.

"That's not what I meant," he whispers, standing, and my head falls back, completely unsurprised that he's choosing to walk away. "I meant for *us*." He says facing me again, zoning in his deep hazel eyes into my stare. Throwing around that word again, like he hasn't abused it. Spat on it, crumpled it up in a ball and threw it in the garbage.

I wait, appreciating the man he is, the time we had briefly before I close off that emotion and turn towards the crack in the pavement again. Shivering as I say the lie that slices the air like the sharpest knife in the arsenal. "There is no us."

Chapter Twenty-Six

Three Weeks Later

ELLE

Devin: please talk to me.

Devin: i'm sorry Elle.

Devin: when do you get back, can we meet for coffee?

Devin: Elle?

Devin: Tell me what to do to make it better. Please? Space, I need space.

I don't know what else to tell Devin over text, so I hit send on the short message that I know will elicit at least two more in return. I have been back in Minnesota for less than a week and I already am so bored and flooded with sorority tasks that I want to go back. Hubert trekked back with me in his airline carrier, and if it wasn't for having to drug him again—just to get him to sleep the short flight without constant wauling— I would already be gone.

Mom spent the first few days telling me about all her friends then the rest showing me all her favorite places where she meets with them.

All of them are nice— don't get me wrong— but obviously they are considerably older and not all so overjoyed that I am a sorority president. Most congratulate me in an odd way, all while others turn up their noses when mom brags about it. It is a common reaction for people who were never a part of a Greek letter organization or had a negative experience of their own.

My email notification pops up and my heart sinks. It's from our delegate at Kappa Sigma Iota headquarters, and the subject isn't pleasant.

Leah calls me a second later.

"Hello?" I say, unsure how to articulate what the contents of the email describe.

"Have you checked your email?"

We both know I have.

"Yes."

"Not exactly a great thing, obviously. You falling below the grade point average required to hold your position."

"What does this mean?"

"Well we have to get it up. I wasn't even aware that grades were posted yet or how someone found out so soon. Since Dakota doesn't have them inputted into the website yet."

"I just got my grades a couple days ago. How do they know?"

"Well that's the thing," she pauses and the static on the phone is palatable, "someone emailed them."

"Who?" My throat constricts.

I click open a new internet tab on my laptop, opening the schools course catalog for winter terms. There's a list of a few two week course electives that fall under my communications degree, and they start in a few days.

"It was reported anonymously." She pauses, and I can hear shuffling on her end of the phone. "Maybe there's an extra class you can take."

"Already looking."

"That's our girl, always a step ahead."

I don't know how to respond so I simply click through the motions to sign up for a leadership communications course called Conflict Management and Leah rambles through all the other items regarding the upcoming Spring Retreat schedule and the correspondence from headquarters regarding our Spring Recruitment themes.

"I have to head back to campus early." I tell mom over dinner. She made us caprese salads but I know she has a box of my favorite ramen in the cupboard for later tonight when I get hungry while reviewing my presentations for the chapter's Spring Retreat.

"Is everything okay?" She looks at me with all the concern a mother can muster, tucking her light brown hair behind her ear as she does.

"Yeah," I shift my fork around my plate. "I signed up for an extra class, to boost my GPA."

"I thought you said you got a 3.5"

"Yeah, well," her response will be the same as always but I continue anyways, "I need a 3.8 to stay being president, all officers are required to hold a higher standard."

"Honey–" she starts.

"Mom, please don't," I huff, "I can't just quit. They are counting on me."

"Okay," she cranes her blue eyes over my face, her lips puckering slightly as she contemplates what to say next. "Is it to see Devin?"

"No, Mom." I exasperate, dramatically. " I told you we weren't together like that."

"I know. I know I just thought maybe it was just sex."

"Mom!" I shake my head, my cheeks flush hot, spreading the blush all over my face, "like I said we aren't together anymore."

"Are you going to see your dad before you leave?"

"No." I say quickly, my stomach churning at the thought. I place my fork down and chug the rest of my water. "I have to send an email."

"I'm not gonna push you, honey, but maybe—"

"He didn't want me." I say, standing with my bowl painted with the remains of balsamic vinegar across it.

"Well I'm not sure what to say to that, but don't shut him out just because I did."

"I don't shut him out, he chose to stop responding, reaching out, and generally speaking to me unless it's convenient for him, so I can't. I am too busy."

"Okay." She continues eating her mozzarella and tomatoes as I make my way to the kitchen and clean my bowl before storing it in the dishwasher.

"You can tell me that stuff you know." She hollers from the dining room.

"I know." I respond, evening my tone. She doesn't want us to have a strangled relationship, we spent the better half of my teens at odds like most daughters and mothers, but after the divorce she transformed into more of a friend than a parent— navigating that relationship has been interesting to say the least— but we are getting better at it with every month and year that passes.

I contemplate getting more wine, but decide otherwise, placing my short stemmed glass in the upper rack of the dishwasher next to my cleaned bowl. Then slipping on the gloves to wash off the chef's knife, cutting board, and other dishes that have piled up in the sink from the day. Mom brings her dishes in and I rinse those as well, before filling the dishwasher and close it. Mom waits a moment before opening her arms and embracing me.

"I want you, you know." She whispers into my hair.

"I know. I want you too." I say into her shoulder.

Chapter Twenty-Seven

First day of Spring Semester

DEVIN

"It's called the Nightingale and I can't wait to read it honestly." Jinny says, hosting up the blue book with a wool gloved hand. We just spent all of the past Sunday before classes began in a bookstore in downtown Conifer Valley.

"Historical Fiction. Sounds like your kind of book." I reply, scanning every face we pass on campus. Today's Jinny's first day, and I don't mind leading her to class. I just also hope that the building she has English Lit. in also housed a specific communications students classes as well.

The snow has already melted away from the paved sidewalk, and the moisture is being sucked up by the heat of the rising sun— creating a mist around our feet as we trudge up the hill. Passing the library clock tower as it strikes ten.

I don't have class until later this afternoon, but Jinny has four of them back to back for the next few hours.

"So we will meet in the dining hall I showed you for dinner?"

"I actually have plans tonight." Jinny stops her ascent up the hill, and scans my face. Her bright pink nose and freckles are all on full display as she wipes her dirty blonde bangs behind her ear. The rest of her loose curls are in a messy bun. The whole eccentric colored patched sweater paired with her black skirt and even blacker tights all wrapped in a black trench coat is an outfit librarians would envy. At least she is dressing more conservative as the weather remains freezing.

She somehow looks older now, even from a month ago, now that she is an enrolled Conifer Valley University student. Jinny's bright hazel eyes light up at something over my shoulder and I can't help but flinch as she squeals, "Elle!" She shoves past me and assaults Elle in a hug.

I blush creeps over Elles already soft pink cheeks as her sapphire blue eyes meet me and she greets Jinny with a breathtaking smile. Then she's hugging Jinny back, unlike I thought she ever would. Jinny is overly eccentric and huggy— Elle not so much, but she lets it happen nonetheless.

"Hi." I say, entranced by her presence.

"Hi." she responds, breaking our eye contact to scan Jinny. Jinny holds firm to her elbow as she pulls her off to the side of the path and begins expressing her excitement for being at Conifer Valley and begging for them to exchange numbers. Before whispering something in Elle's ear that I can't interpret with her back to me, but Elle smiles and nods so I relax my shoulders.

I told Jinny what happened, and she lectured me heavily about it— I'm sure I'll get another round soon— but she looks at Elle now with nothing but admiration. I can't help but stare at the pair of them, until the urge to kick Jinny off Elle overwhelms me.

"Okay J, off to class." I say, tugging her arm and shoving her up the hill with a gentle but firm hand. "You don't want to be late."

"Text me." Jinny instructs Elle, but does not hesitate to walk herself the rest of the way up to the warmth of the building.

"Hi." I say again, instantly horrified that I am repeating myself.

"You said that."

"Yeah," I clear my throat and gesture a hand towards the coffee cart a few strides in front of us. There's a small line but I welcome any stall of our departure from one another. "Coffee?"

"Sure, but I'm buying."

"Deal." I say, smiling widely at her default reaction.

"How are you?" I ask as she says "did you have a good break?"

"Good." She says, as we step up in the line.

"Yeah, I stayed here. What about you? How was Minnesota?"

"Freezing, but I had to come back early for a winter class." She says, then orders her coffee. Black, and I do the same.

"That's great." I say, unsure what else to say.

"Yeah, I have to focus more on classes, my GPA got pretty low after last semester."

There's a pause that feels all too awkward, so I jump to fill it again as we reach for our coffees, slapping lids on them as we tuck them in their cardboard koozies.

"These are great inventions." I say, regretting the weird comment immediately.

"Yeah," she laughs, and the sound causes my stomach to lurch. "They're so you don't burn your hands."

"Makes sense." We sit on the bench near the top of the slope and watch as a few students enter the double doors into the building ahead of us. The coffee warms our hands– even through the cardboard contraption— but far too hot to sip just yet.

"Elle," I start, expecting her to stop me like she did the last time we found ourselves sitting in the same formation at the end of last semester. When she doesn't, I continue, "I never apologized properly."

"You mean with dinner?" she says and my brows force themselves together, "or is that only for when you punch a girl in the nose."

I laugh at the jab. "No, I meant I wasn't in the best headspace that day to apologize for not telling you in advance that I was asked to convince you to—"

"I forgive you." She interrupts me before I can dive too far into the semantics of our fight. "I'm sorry, too. We were both in a crazy head space and we got sucked into this whirlwind of–"

"Fun?" I offer.

"Lust, was the word I was going to use."

"I prefer not to complicate it." I shrug, testing the hot liquid of my coffee on my tongue and it burns my taste buds slightly.

"Everything in Greek life is a little complicated unfortunately," she says, her gaze scanning the crowds walking by again.

"Too many social pressures and all that." I offer, sipping my coffee again, and burning my numb tongue further.

"Something like that."

"Can we start over?" I ask, reaching for her hand, and she opens her palm to accept the gesture. My heart hums rapidly until I meet her eyes again. The blue in them is as striking as the day we met, but somehow filled with so much more emotion.

"I need to focus on me this semester. School, the sorority, all of it."

"Right." I say accepting this fact, but hating every bit of it with all of my being.

"Crazy that Jinny's here." She says squeezing my hand.

"Yeah, she's already ditching me tonight for something more important."

"Ah," she nods, and the knowing smile she gives me fills me with trepidation.

"What?"

"She asked me for a recommendation letter for KSI."

"When?" I say, stunned that Jinny never mentioned wanting to join a sorority to me.

"Just now." She laughs.

"Are you going to write her one?"

"I don't need to write a letter, I'll just tell the recruitment chair, but if a letter helps her feel better of course I'll write one." She explains, and my haunches lower again. This is good Devin, chill.

"You'd do that for her."

"If she's anything like you expressed we'd be idiots not to let her in, but she still has to attend the events for recruitment. She's most likely already planning to go to the open house tonight. Since you mentioned she has plans."

I nod, wondering where I missed the signs, if I missed them, but all of that quickly fades away as Elle continues telling me about how her and her mom went to a zoo light event in Minneapolis when she was home.

I watch her in rapt content over being able to speak to her, and listen to her laugh. Even though she's drawn a line in the sand between us for now. The crowds thin around us, and our coffees cool with the weather.

We sit in the chill and converse until the class hour ends and she never lets go of my hand.

Chapter Twenty-Eight

A Not So Random Friday in March

ELLE

"Elle, we are ready for you." Leah states from the door.

I am the only one in the hall. Word travelled like wildfire throughout the chapter when I submitted my application for another term— and like Leah and I expected, no other member applied in opposition. What I didn't tell Leah was that I was slightly disappointed by that fact.

The election committee is all friendly faces, and the questions are toss ups, but nothing unexpected. I can validate my faults from the previous term and explain my routes of differing approaches if the issues are to occur again. None of them even seem worried. Which triggers something in me.

"Who would you select if not me?" I ask, and though I know the statement is bold I don't think they understand why I ask it.

"The constitution says we would choose a selection of candidates to apply, hoping one of them feels encouraged to interview." Jordan— the sister in charge of the election committee is one I don't know very well, but she was the previous social media chair from the executive council and came into her position with a heavy recommendation from Laura— states from the head of the table. "Why?" she narrows her green eyes on me and I can't help but smile back at her.

"Well I actually would like to withdraw my application." I say, and the sister next to my with striking features and deep brown hair– I think her name is Raven— gasps. Only making me smile widen.

"What?" Leah straighteners her spine and shoots me a concerned look. She hasn't spoken this entire time.

"I didn't intend for the dramatics, and honestly walking in here I thought there was no other option, most likely like the rest of you. I appreciate all the support in this term, and I wouldn't change it for the world, but I think the chapter will blossom under another's head instead."

"Do you have someone in mind?" Evy, a smaller sister with large rimmed glasses and ombre hair, asks politely.

"Actually, yes." I smile, leaning forward on my elbows. "Laura. I can explain why, but I'm sure you all know all of her strengths."

"She doesn't want to," pipes up Luna— Laura's little— as I expected.

"I know, but I plan to speak to her." I express, "and I'd like the chance to advise her directly if possible, since I'll still be a member of the chapter, but I don't need to hold a position. I actually need to focus on school a bit more, and would like to bond better with my sisters."

I don't get to be a part of the discussion further, and honestly the fresh air or the idea of having less to stress about next year seems to cleanse me. I can finally go home for the summer without feeling tied to everything back here, I can bond deeper with Frankie and Hillary. The idea of our friendship making it past the executive board roles causes the next breath to come out full of hope. I also will have more time to dedicate to the virtual therapy I signed up for.

My phone pings and I notice it's an email from Holden. The title indicates he has a job opportunity for me. I scan through the request to meet him in his office at one of the provided times, asking me to officially interview for the student life offices Special Events Planner position.

He states in the email that the job hours can be adjusted based on my student schedule and sorority events, and that I will get paid an amount equivalent to the state's minimum wage per hour worked. I had no idea a position like this existed, let alone had an opening. A job sounds absolutely perfect at this very moment, since my time was now my own to spend. At least after the final meeting I'll head at the beginning of May.

Finally I'll be me next semester. Their sister, and hopefully their friend. A student with a real job, working towards paying for the chapter. A normal junior in college— working on finishing school in the next few years. Being a big sister worthy of the name, not just another authority figure for the chapter to avoid, a girl with normal collegiate issues, not heavy adult leveled drama.

A person— not just a sorority president.

ELLE

"**W**hat time is our flight tomorrow?" I yell through the open bedroom door. Waiting a few silent seconds before I continue. "Devin? What time do I need to be ready?"

"We have to leave at noon." Devin's deep voice carries from the lower story of our home. The old Victorian wood creaks as he begins climbing the stairs. He most likely is holding a basket of laundry, because he just decided what to pack.

I, on the other hand, have been packing and repacking my bag for the last week. You'd think after our third time planning for a trip to Iceland that I would know how many coats to pack, and how many layers I would need for a month away from home.

"Are my wool socks in that load?" I ask as Devin enters our master bedroom— the plastic white holed basket of laundry in his arms. He has filled out since we first met in college all those years ago. He still has the same dirty blonde hair, and even though it's longer it still falls in a natural way that I can only explain as "super sexy". His hazel eyes trace over me before he sets the basket on the bed and dumps the mound of clothes onto it. The soft white duvet scattered with colors of freshly dried garments.

"I see one, two, three," he pauses and my hands start to gather a shirt before shaking it out and laying it flat towards one side of the bed. "Four socks."

"No I need my wool ones," I say, throwing down another shirt, starting to pile them on top of one another before shuffling my bare feet to our walk-in closet. "Did you find your wind breaker?"

"Yes," Devin says, while looking at his phone as he also separates our laundry with one hand.

"What's wrong?"

"Nothing." He says, setting his phone on the nightstand, "I just had an email from the company owner that I wanted to respond to before I forgot."

"Are you sure they are okay with you working from Reykjavik for a month?"

"Yes, Your Highness." Devin hums the nickname he assigned me so long ago with a smile on his lips.

I dig through the drawer I keep my socks in before finding one pair of my wool socks. The other pair must still be in the laundry somewhere.

"Rory!" I hollow down the hallway, "Are you packed yet?"

Silence welcomes me, not unlike her father, Rory requires me to ask her questions twice. "Rory, honey?"

"Yes, mom!" Replies our thirteen year old daughter, matching her father in more ways than one as her fingers fly across her cellphone while she walks into the hall from her room across from ours.

"Did you pack the outfit we bought the other day?" I ask to meet her in the middle of the hall, tucking a hair behind her ear as it falls into her face. "Because you know we are taking our family pictures again in the same spot as last time.

"Yes, I did." Rory's eyes meet mine and they sparkle with golden flecks just like her fathers.

"Perfect thank you, honey." I say, as she steps around me to head down the stairs. "Find the menu for that Ramen place, we don't have anything in the fridge for dinner since we're leaving tomorrow."

She doesn't respond, heavily invested in her phone, but I don't care, because Rory is the perfect daughter. Our only, after a long run of attempting to have as many as possible but running into some infertility problems after I birthed her. After many years and multiple diagnosis we decided three family members was our fate.

I run my fingers over the table at the top of the stairs, admiring the metal city themed photos frame— each city's frame decorated with the most popular attractions. Inside each one is a photo of either Devin and I before Rory was born or the three of us after she was gifted to us. New York when Devin and I graduated from Conifer Valley, the two of us in Iceland for our wedding, then the three of us in France when Rory was two. Many more with our famed Iceland trip that started up again when Rory was five. All our memories amongst the dozen or so frames we have collected over the years.

"You're gorgeous, you know that?" My eyes find Devin as he leans— arms and ankles crossed— on the thick boards of the door frame. The morning light is casting him in a glorious glow and the smile I feel inch onto my face is genuine. It's one that I have taken years to master but now it's the most natural feeling in the world when I am happy. Married to my best friend for the last decade and a half and about to celebrate our anniversary with a month abroad. Just the three of us.

Devin uncrosses his limbs and hikes a thumb over his shoulder, "Now, are you gonna help me with our laundry or not?"

I can't help but laugh as I reach him and he swoops me under his arm before tugging me around to face him. I wrap my arms around his torso and inhale the scent of him— vanilla just like our shared shampoo and conditioner (well my shampoo, that he often steals), before he places a delicate kiss to the tip of my nose.

"I love you so much." I say.

"I love you more." He says.

"I love you most," pride flushing through me at the fact that I am the one who got the last sentence this time.

Acknowledgements

To all my sorority sisters, across all the years I was in Phi Sigma Sigma, I'm sorry I learned almost a decade later that I could've been a better sister at the foundation. This project started as a way for me to sift through all the unprocessed trauma I stuffed down in the years I was growing into being a woman. I loved many of you so deeply and the severance of the relationships and the drifting of contact has shown me that people are like waves. All are impactful, but some are far larger and stronger than others. I learned so much from all of you, and I know that the ones who decide to read this thinking it was going to be a slash piece might be a bit disappointed. But for those of you who opened the cover with the same admiration you held for me back then, thank you. I never felt truly worthy of all your support but appreciate it all the same.

Never forget to Aim High ladies!

xoxo

To my beloved husband, Aaron, thank you for staying by my side from the day I decided to join the sorority, through every hardship, crying session, and overall every year following. Especially, when I spent almost a decade figuring out who I was, and never faltering or losing faith in me. Even when I will inevitably change course again—because what is life without a little adventure!

Meet the Author

Audrianna was president of her sororities chapter at The University of Colorado Springs in Colorado Springs for two consecutive years. She held other positions before and after her terms and credits a majority of her work ethic and social skills to being apart of the Greek community. With out which she wouldn't have been able to make connections that landed many of her jobs, and granted her a life long friendship, along with many life lessons.

She married her high school sweet heart right after they graduated from college. They spent their early 20's traveling across Europe. Then, in the early months of 2023 they welcomed their beautiful baby girl. Granting them a tiny travel companion, who has already been to Iceland at the age of 9 months as well as France and Italy at 2 years old.

Through the years, Audrianna has dabbled in many creative worlds, from culinary arts, to marketing, all the way to writing Adult Novels. Her trio of friends is never far. Having grown up with her two best friends, and maintaining those relationships through adult hood, has helped her through all of the times when she's felt a little lost.

Also by Audrianna M. Brownell

The Rise of a Visionary: Book one in the Lost Isle Collection

Upcoming Books

Check out the Authors website!

https://novelsbyamb.com/